MR. SINCLAIR
BEGUILES
A BLUESTOCKING

SOFIE DARLING

OLIVERHEBERBOOKS

Chapter One

29 December 1818

Miss Violet Hotchkiss never expected to walk into Sir John and Lady Sinclair's evening soirée and fall headlong into love.

Indeed, one would hardly expect it of a bespectacled wallflower of four and twenty years who was more comfortable discussing the 1815 Corn Law than the latest in ladies' fashion.

And yet, she had.

Only minutes earlier, Violet had been alighting from her parents' carriage and bracing against the wintry cold with her burgundy velvet cloak wrapped tight about her, prepared for the usual sort of supper party, with all the usual local gentry.

She stopped to adjust her spectacles, which had slipped down her nose.

"Violet." Her sister Lily rushed from her carriage, breath puffing white through the smile curving her mouth. Everyone had always agreed that of the Hotchkiss sisters Lily had the prettiest smile. It was an opinion with which Violet wholeheartedly agreed.

Lily's arm twined through Violet's. "Is Mr. Granville attending?" Violet asked. Only last summer Lily had become Mrs. Charles Granville. Violet still hadn't fully adjusted to the idea of her beloved sister being a *Mrs.*

Lily used her fan to point out the small grouping behind them. "Charles is asking for Papa's advice regarding an agricultural matter." Lily leaned in conspiratorially. "I think he does it so Papa will think well of him." Lily's gaze flew upward and roved over the house before them. "Isn't Somerton Manor splendidly lovely?"

Constructed of light gray stone, Somerton Manor was an elegant, rectangular house with few pediments and plain pilasters framing the front door. Perfectly symmetrical and English, it was indisputably the finest house in the neighborhood, not including the Earl and Countess of Holland's magnificent estate, Welles Castle, which Violet didn't include as she only saw it once a year at their annual Twelfth Night Ball.

Violet gave a noncommittal murmur. It wasn't that she disagreed with Lily's observation. It was that her sister had made it at all. Lily had only begun commenting on other people's houses after she'd become a married gentlelady. Violet was learning that the wedded state changed women in ways ineffable and mysterious. How lucky that she would never marry.

They took the staircase at a quick clip; such was the motivating factor of the biting wind. Of course, it was exactly the sort of night one would expect in late December. Besides, one couldn't hold the cold against such a beautiful, clear night with the stars winking their twinkly brilliance above.

At the top, the front door swung open on smooth hinges to usher them into the inviting warmth beyond. Although Somerton Manor was a grand house from the outside, Violet had always appreciated that its interior was built to be lived in, with its downstairs of warm oak-paneled rooms that instantly made one feel cozy and at home.

After leaving their cloaks with a footman, Violet and Lily continued into the main hall, where Sir John and Lady Sinclair were receiving their guests. "If it isn't the most lovely Mrs. Granville and the most erudite Miss Hotchkiss," said Sir John with his familiar, paternal wink.

Violet smiled agreeably, even as she sighed on the inside. *Of course.*

In her thirteenth year, she'd been found shortsighted

and fitted for her first pair of spectacles. In an instant, she'd gone from being a *pretty-enough girl* to *well-read* and *bookish*. *Erudite* was simply a variation on the theme. *Bluestocking* was yet another, but in a few years one word would surpass all others. *Spinster*, a word that would stick with her all the rest of her days.

Spinsterhood was the inevitable fate of well-read, bookish, erudite bluestockings, a fact that had become clear to her as their family, friends, and acquaintances had separated her and Lily into intelligent and lovely, respectively. So, Violet had taken the persona yoked onto her, tried it on for size, and found it fit, mostly. She enjoyed books and learning. If on occasion she viewed her sister's life and experienced a pang of envy, it passed quickly, for she loved Lily with all her heart and begrudged her nothing.

Although, it must be admitted that a certain question did sometimes poke its sharp, little point into her: Why was that life closed off to a well-read, bookish, erudite bluestocking? It was as if the possibility never occurred to anyone else, therefore everyone expected it would never occur to her. It was easier to throw herself into books. Besides, she'd never once met a gentleman who compared to the hero of one.

"Sir John, Lady Sinclair," Lily said, "what a perfect night for a soirée."

"We simply had to celebrate Sinclair's return to us," said Lady Sinclair, as if she couldn't quite believe the fact herself.

"Returned alive and all in one piece, I might add," chimed Sir John on a laugh that contained a note of seriousness.

Sinclair ... Will Sinclair, Sir John and Lady Sinclair's only child, had come home after three years of travels to this and that exotic locale, clearly to the relief of his parents who had dutifully kept their neighbors apprised of his latest jaunts. Lily offered her happy congratulations, and Violet smiled along. It wasn't that she wished any harm on Sinclair. It was simply that she'd never had any doubt that he would return home, alive, and in one piece. Sinclair had always seemed a capable sort.

Sir John craned his neck around and began glancing about the hall. "Now where has the boy got off to?" But his search was cut short when Violet and Lily's parents, Mr. and Mrs. Hotchkiss, entered the hall with Mr. Granville. Now the host and hostess were on to further greetings.

Lily tugged Violet's arm. "Come with me," she said, sotto voce. "I have news to share."

Violet experienced a frisson equal parts excitement and dread. Since Lily's wedding, Violet had been expecting *news*. Once ensconced in a quiet corner of the drawing room, Lily grabbed both of Violet's hands and squeezed. "Can you guess my news?"

"Oh, sister," Violet said, sudden tears springing to her eyes, "I am overcome with joy for you." And she was. She truly, truly was. "But you shall give me a niece first. Then you can have all the boys you like."

"Vivi," Lily began on a laugh, "how you do love to control matters. But even you cannot influence this outcome."

Violet's responding smirk did the job of suppressing the familiar pang of envy. Once she'd understood she would never marry, she'd accepted she would never have children. Lily, the younger sister by two years, had been the one destined for marriage, so the sisters had begged that they be allowed to debut together. Their parents hadn't been able to deny the wisdom of such an arrangement and assented. At their debut dance, Mr. Granville had been first to sweep Lily across the dancing floor, and her future had been set.

"Come," Lily began, pulling Violet forward, "let us be social. Who has arrived?"

Violet gave the room a quick once-over. "The Baring-Whites are here. And Mrs. Acton."

"Did Mrs. Baring-White bring her spaniel?"

"One must wonder if she is allowed to leave her house without it."

Lily flashed Violet an impish grin. How Violet loved to pull that grin from her sister. They didn't much need words to communicate.

Across the room, Mr. Granville gave Lily a nearly imperceptible nod. Lily's smile transformed into one entirely inscrutable to Violet. She was no longer the only person in the world with whom Lily didn't need words to communicate. It had taken a bit of getting used to.

Drawn by the magnetic force of her husband, Lily pulled a slightly annoyed Violet along. As they joined the group, Papa was saying with an affable smile, "So, that vagabond son of yours is done traveling the world?"

Sir John beamed. "I am happy to confirm all the reports are true. Sinclair is home to stay." He gave his longtime neighbor a clap on the back. "Though I've had a devil of a time keeping an eye on the boy tonight. Mayhap Quincy will know."

"Quincy?" asked Mama. Like any attentive mother of a marriageable daughter, her ear was ever attuned to the mention of a gentleman. After all, he could be moneyed and unmarried. "Who is Quincy?"

"Mr. Oliver Quincy is my beloved sister's son," explained Lady Sinclair. "He is paying us a brief visit on his way up to Town."

The tension released from Mama's shoulders. "So, he is a good sort?" she asked, relentless.

Violet glanced at Lily, so they could share a private laugh, but Lily's attention was fixed and doting upon Mr. Granville.

"Quincy is a fine young man, to be sure." Sir John cast his gaze about the room. "Ah, and there he is."

Violet followed along with everyone else to locate the young gentleman. Her heart did a funny little pitter-pat in her chest. Never once in its four and twenty years had her heart behaved so.

As he navigated toward them, one couldn't help but be taken by Mr. Quincy's elegance of bearing and learned air. He was of a middling height that wasn't too tall, with fine dark hair that lay in a perfect coif and large dark eyes that conveyed the sense that they weren't too impressed by his surroundings. A man could not be too learned, but he could be too impressed. Violet had never observed a man who so precisely personified an artist's rendering of the perfect English gentleman.

"Sir John, you desire my presence?" asked Mr. Quincy. Even the studiously enunciated syllables of his voice were just as they should be.

"Come and meet Mr. and Mrs. Hotchkiss, my boy," said Sir John.

"Delighted," said Mr. Quincy as he bowed over Mama's hand.

"And their family, Mr. and Mrs. Granville," Sir John continued.

Mr. Quincy bowed over Lily's hand. "Charmed."

"And Miss Hotchkiss."

Mr. Quincy turned to Violet. A hot flush rose inside her, and her heart was off to the races. "Enchanted," he spoke over her hand.

Violet had difficulty drawing breath. *Enchanted?* She had never enchanted anyone in her entire life. A breathy "Oh," escaped her in the form of an exhale that may have ended in a bit of a giggle.

Lily cut her a sharp glance, and Violet attempted to remember herself. She wasn't the sort of young lady who giggled.

"Ah, there is Sinclair." Sir John smiled, his eyes alight with pride and affection.

Once again, as one they followed the direction of his pleased smile as Sinclair approached from the opposite end of the room, politely avoiding various groupings vying for his attention.

"Oh, my, but his travels seem to have agreed with him," murmured Mama.

"Indeed," came Lily's breathy reply. Mr. Granville lifted an eyebrow at the appreciation in his wife's voice.

Violet and Sinclair were of a similar age, with him being two years her elder, and as their families were friendly neighbors, they had grown up in the way those of friendly proximity did—seeing each other about the village, at general assemblies, at teas and fêtes. Although Sir John was a baronet, he'd never lorded that fact about the neighborhood. Still, Violet had always kept her distance from Sinclair. For all they'd grown up in the same environ, he'd always discomfited her.

His height had been too towering. His shoulders too massive. His face too handsome. He had been quite simply *too* everything.

And now, he was still in possession of these qualities, yet somehow different, as if a sharper edge ran along the length of him. She couldn't help wondering what had forged this new quality that rendered him even more forbidding, but she dismissed the curiosity in favor of a safer man to think upon: Mr. Quincy. He was a man who wasn't *too* anything.

Of a sudden, a fitting comparison between these two men struck Violet. Mr. Quincy fit the ideal of the perfect hero from a novel with his smooth, refined features. And Will Sinclair? Well, he would be the rake, a man whose overwhelming handsomeness and slightly brutish exterior many a lady would find impossible to resist.

Sinclair first greeted Mr. and Mrs. Hotchkiss, as was

proper. Mama's cheeks looked a trifle flushed as she returned his felicitations. Next, he turned to Mr. and Mrs. Granville, congratulating them on their summer nuptials.

During this time, Violet had taken a great interest in the seams of her satin gloves. Then she felt them: eyes upon her. Sinclair's, she knew it. He possessed one of those gazes that was ever unflinching.

Once the silence had gone on a beat too long, she relented and met his deep blue eyes. Perplexingly, her breath caught in her lungs and refused to be reasonable and release. She felt strange and exposed, as if Sinclair could see down to the cockles of her soul. She didn't remember this about him.

Sir John cleared his throat. "Miss Hotchkiss, you'll remember Sinclair?"

Sinclair's eyebrows drew together in confusion. "*Miss* Hotchkiss?" he asked.

Violet had forgotten how deep his voice was. *Too* deep.

All eyes swung toward her. She forced an uneasy laugh. She never did enjoy being at the center of a gathering's attention. "That has been my name these last four and twenty years," she chirped lightly, which did nothing to dispel the scowl on Sinclair's face.

"But how is it you're unwed?" he asked.

Violet blinked.

Had he truly asked such a question? In company?

He had.

She opened her mouth and closed it, flummoxed and speechless for the first time in her life.

Chapter Two

It wasn't the charged beat of silence following his question which convinced Will that he'd truly stepped in it. It was the parade of emotions that marched across Miss Hotchkiss's face.

First shock, which seemed reasonable, in all honesty. Then a quick flash of outrage, followed by a longer moment of confusion. When her features at last settled, bewilderment was what remained.

"Sometimes one is presented with other choices," she said, her voice gone rigid and tight.

An implication lay within her words that had Will's brow furrowing. Had she the choice? And, more importantly, did she want it?

In truth, he'd expected to return to England and find

Miss Violet Hotchkiss married to a local landowner with one child in leading strings and a second one on the way.

Instead, here she stood before him, unattached.

He shouldn't feel anything about it. But he couldn't contain a small reaction of relief, which he immediately tamped down.

"Now," began Sir John, "I have it on good authority that we shall dine ten minutes hence. Is that correct, Lady Sinclair?"

Mother nodded before picking up her pug dog, Mr. Rascal, who had started whining at her ankles. She ever had a pug or two running around.

"Dining ten minutes hence?" came Oliver Quincy's uniquely high-pitched voice as he made a show of consulting his pocket watch. "At eight of the clock?"

Of all Will's cousin's, Quincy might have been his least favorite. It was the sheer pomposity with which he carried himself that made it impossible to actually enjoy his company.

"Such an early dining time," Quincy continued, unable to help himself once he got going on a subject, "would be unforgivably unfashionable in London."

"Bless the heavens we are not in London, then," chimed Mrs. Acton from her seat by the fire. Well into her dotage—the woman had to be eighty, if a day—Mrs.

Acton had grown rather frail over the last few years, but she'd retained all her firm opinions and the pluck to voice them.

Her assertion came as the permission everyone in the room needed to break into laughter and relief. Indeed, this wasn't London. This was the country, where they could be free from such constraints and silliness and eat at a reasonable hour. This was the message their laughter conveyed. And Quincy, who was now carefully winding his watch, noticed not one bit.

Anticipation of the meal added a spark to the air as everyone began milling about, groupings forming and reforming in different configurations. As Sir John's son, Will understood his duty was to circulate and make their guests, who represented the best families in the neighborhood—save the Earl and Countess of Holland, who were a bit grand for this more intimate gathering—feel welcome. He'd known them nearly all his life, and someday it would be he who played host to these gatherings. It was why he'd come home. To do his duty and fill his role.

But it didn't mean he had to mingle with all his guests. Take Miss Hotchkiss, for example. He wouldn't go near her. The only problem was that the periphery of his vision had no such reservations.

She hadn't substantially changed from the young lady he'd last seen three years ago when he'd gone off on the Grand Tour that had taken a year longer than expected. She was possessed of the same small, lithe figure. Same light brown hair that caught streaks of blond in the summer. Round wire spectacles. And behind those spectacles, a pair of observant blue eyes framed by thick dark lashes. No, her eyes weren't simply blue. *Violet.* Violet Hotchkiss had violet eyes. Eyes that had never once in memory given him the time of day.

Even now, if he happened to catch her gaze, it darted away, leaving him feeling every bit the fool. How was it possible he still carried this youthful infatuation for her after all these years?

The doors to the dining room swung open, and warm light from the two chandeliers and five candelabras set atop the table set for twenty poured into the drawing room. Mother met Will's eye, and he nodded, taking her meaning in an instant. He crossed the room and extended his hand toward Mrs. Acton, who was still seated beside the fire. "May I have the pleasure of escorting you into the dining room?"

The older woman smiled up at him, mischief in her eyes. "I must thank you."

"For what?"

"For helping me realize the best part of being the eldest lady in a gathering," she said as she placed her hand in his.

"And what is that?" Will asked, assisting her to her feet.

"They send a handsome, strapping young man to lead you into dinner."

Will laughed off her flattery as they began their slow progress across the room.

"But might there be a young miss to whom you would rather offer your hand?" Mrs. Acton asked, her bright eyes twinkling with mischief as they landed on none other than Violet Hotchkiss. She patted Will's hand. "No need to worry, my boy, your secret is safe with me."

Will could deny Mrs. Acton's assumption and inform her there was no secret to keep, but she'd lived too long on this earth and seen too much to believe him. Still ... had his affinity for Violet Hotchkiss been obvious to everyone all these years? Further, was a double entendre hidden within her query?

Soon, all were seated at the dining table. As the meal was served and the wine poured, the conversation flowed. It wasn't long before talk turned to the Earl and Countess of Holland's holiday house party and the

Twelfth Night Ball a few days hence. At Will's side, Mrs. Acton chimed in. "What a to-do they put on every year."

"Most impressive," said Sir John, before adding, "and good of them to invite local families."

"For all their London ways," said Mr. Hotchkiss, "no one could accuse the Earl and Countess of thinking themselves too good for their country neighbors."

"Oh, I simply adore their Twelfth Night Ball," said Mrs. Granville.

A similarity between her and Miss Hotchkiss made it apparent they were sisters, but it was Mrs. Granville, with her light blond hair and cornflower blue eyes, who many called the family beauty. Will understood it, even if he couldn't quite agree.

"Truly," Mrs. Granville continued, a dreamy cast to her eye, "'tis my favorite night of the year. All those aristocrats dressed in the latest French fashions and the string quartet brought in from London to play until dawn. One feels so very alive on such a decadent night. Then"—she snapped her fingers—"the next day, life continues on as usual, the next Twelfth Night Ball but three hundred and sixty-four days away."

All this while, Violet, who was seated across and down a few places from Will, partook of her meal and silently attended the conversation around her. He remembered her as a girl and young lady who stated her observations and opinions impetuously, without a care for who heard. Now she appeared more inclined to listen. Even so, Will had no doubt that whatever opinions she held, they were firmly formed inside her head.

"But, oh, the tattle coming out of the Earl and Countess's house party this year," inserted Mrs. Baring-White. "There will be scandal. Mark my words."

"It's the young ladies these days." Mrs. Acton heaved mournful sigh. "I dare say, the ideas they get in their heads. I place the blame squarely on the head of all those Gothic novels."

Through dessert, chatter about the Holland house party continued until it was time to return to the large drawing room, the elders claiming the central grouping of sofas and chairs near the fire and the younger people grouped together near the globe on the library end of the room. Will knew his father would like him to stay with the elders and properly reintroduce himself into their society. With a slight pang, that was what he did, even though his heart wasn't in it.

"Sinclair," asked Mr. Hotchkiss, "how does it feel to be living beneath the family roof again?"

Will was opening his mouth to respond when his mother said, "Actually, Mr. Hotchkiss, Sinclair isn't truly living beneath our roof."

Mrs. Hotchkiss gave a little frown. "Oh?"

Will cleared his throat. "I am residing in the estate's cottage."

Sir John gave a jolly laugh. "Sinclair was always a lad possessed of an independent mind. But now he's taken his rightful place at Somerton, learning its workings."

"How do you find the occupation?" This from Mr. Baring-White.

"I enjoy it," Will found himself saying and, surprisingly, meaning every word. He'd determined long ago to be a useful man, having no interest in the wastrel London life of his peers. Like his cousin Quincy, for example.

In truth, Will had been relieved when he returned from his travels and found Father keen on him sharing in the running of the estate. Will had had but one request: that he be able to take up a separate residence in the cottage house.

Once the men separated into a discussion about animal husbandry, Will discreetly extricated himself from the group and ambled toward the library end. Although he was still too far away to hear the details, he gathered the discourse was bright and lively.

Quincy caught Will's eye and beckoned him over.

Will settled uncomfortably into a too upright chair and listened in silence.

"True gentlemen do not have time for novels," Quincy stated in apparent continuation of the ongoing conversation.

Miss Hotchkiss's eyebrows drew together. "No?"

"They are naught more than piffle for the silly minded."

Will expected Miss Hotchkiss to roundly contradict Quincy. He quite looked forward to it, in fact, for her voracious reading habit was well known. His cousin could use a good setting down.

But she didn't. Instead, she closed her mouth, looking both chastised and intrigued by Quincy.

A bad feeling began to churn in Will's gut. Next thing, he opened his mouth and said, "I read novels." Four sets of wide eyes turned on him. He went on. "That Henry Fielding chap wrote one that I enjoyed immensely."

Miss Hotchkiss's eyebrows further crinkled together. *"The History of Tom Jones?"*

"Cousin," Quincy said in the tone that so grated on Will's nerves, "that book is hardly the subject for mixed company. Further, it only serves to illustrate my point."

Will had long been tolerant of Quincy's propensity toward self-importance, but tonight it truly irked. Miss

Hotchkiss, however, didn't seem to have heard Quincy's chastisement and for once was staring directly at Will. "You don't read novels."

She said it with such certainty that Will took no small amount of satisfaction in holding her violet eyes captive and contradicting her. "But I do."

She blinked first.

"Vivi," asked Mrs. Granville, "will you be able to make your morning book deliveries to Bumpstead Hollow after such a late night tonight?"

"Book deliveries?" Quincy asked.

"Oh, yes, Violet has a little library of books that she circulates between the local children every Tuesday."

"To what end?" Quincy looked thoroughly befuddled. For himself, Will felt genuine interest stir.

"They do rather enjoy them," Miss Hotchkiss said. "And they learn to read."

Will didn't like the defensive tone in her voice. She sounded ... meek. When had Violet Hotchkiss become *meek*?

"Oh, you'll not dissuade her," Mrs. Granville said. "She feels quite passionately about it."

When Quincy opened his mouth to no doubt pontificate at length on his views about education for the masses, Will said, "Everyone should be free to pursue their passion."

Miss Hotchkiss's wide eyes rounded on him. Then she blushed.

He'd made Violet Hotchkiss blush. A first. A frisson of pleasure traced through him.

As the conversation returned to the scandalous house party underway but a few miles distant, Will considered Miss Hotchkiss's reaction to his assertion. Her library was her passion. Will understood something about this. Once he'd a passion of his own, for charcoal and paintbrush and for creating art. When Will had broached the subject of pursuing the discipline at university, Sir John had informed him in no uncertain terms that this was a passion unsuitable for the only son of landed gentry.

So, Will had gone to Christ Church College at Oxford and, like many young gentlemen of his class, studied classics with a concentration in rowing and downing pints of beer. He'd excelled at those pursuits, particularly the rowing.

It was only when Miss Hotchkiss's mouth tipped up into a smile that Will realized he'd been staring at the side of her face. He followed the direction of her gaze and found who she was so entirely concentrated upon.

Oliver Quincy. The dunderhead was now pontificating at length about the superiority of London life over the country. How could Violet Hotchkiss possibly find his cousin so interesting?

As soon as Will asked himself the question, the answer came to him.

Oh.

He blinked, hoping to see a different expression on her face when he opened his eyes. But, no, her adoring gaze was unmistakable.

Violet Hotchkiss harbored a tendre for Quincy.

Quincy?

It was simply that since Will had been a lad, Violet Hotchkiss had been his ideal. She was bright, intelligent, and spirited, and she'd never had an ounce of use for him. That she had any use for Quincy, well, that was mystifying. Will had always thought those keen eyes of hers could cut through a person and see them down to skin and bone.

How would a milksop like Quincy even know what to do with a woman like Violet Hotchkiss?

Clearly, though, she didn't share Will's point of view.

Right.

With sudden decision, he shot to his feet. "I must ensure the carriage is readied to carry Mrs. Acton home."

Not one minute later, Will was beneath the starry

winter sky and striding toward the stable, the crunch of gravel the only sound in the still night. He determined to put Violet Hotchkiss behind him. Clearly, she adored another.

And if that man was Oliver Quincy, well, Will would find a way to make his peace with it.

Even if it did heat his blood to a near boil.

Chapter Three

Finished with her fifth book delivery of the day, Violet stepped onto the high street of Bumpstead Hollow and snugged deeply into her woolen cloak. With the previous night's clear sky, the morning was a bitingly cold one.

In the household she'd just left, young Ben Wilkes was making great strides with his reading. Possessed of an insatiable curiosity and a mind that absorbed every bit of information it took in, the boy could easily advance his education beyond the village school. If his family allowed him. It was the sticking point that Violet found difficult to accept, even if she did understand it. For many families, all hands were needed to put food on the table. When the time came, perhaps Violet could facilitate an apprenticeship for the boy.

With only the final delivery remaining, she came to the edge of the cobblestone walk and gave the street a cursory check up and down for traffic. There, in the distance, with the sun at his back, came a lone rider on a magnificent chestnut bay, sitting his mount with utter ease. *Sinclair.*

Violet stuttered to an inelegant stop. Then she took a distracted step forward but forgot the low step that separated the cobblestone walk from the street. In an instant, her skirts, cloak, and books were flying about her as she took a clumsy tumble.

"Oh!" she cried as she landed hard on her hands and knees, books scattered all around her. She could blame the sun in her eyes, but she knew the truth.

She'd become distracted by Will Sinclair. Some might see him on his mount and declare him glorious—in fact, Lily had once made that exact observation—but Violet made it a definite point *not* to indulge in Will Sinclair's glory.

Except, just now, it was possible she had.

And she'd lost her footing.

Right.

Next thing she knew, he was beside her, gathering up the books with great efficiency. Embarrassment streaked through Violet. Sinclair must think her the clumsiest oaf who ever walked the earth. She was annoyed with the man, although for what precisely she couldn't quite say. Mayhap for making her senses become all jumbled by his very presence. Last night, it'd been her breath that had gone unreasonable at the sight of him. Today, it was her feet, too.

Refusing his extended hand, Violet picked herself up from the ground and dusted off her skirts. It was only when she stood facing Sinclair that she realized he held all her books. She extended her arms. "I'll be needing those."

"This is quite an armful," was all he said in that deep baritone of his. He hadn't moved a muscle to make the transfer.

Violet huffed a short, sharp breath. "They are nothing I cannot manage." She waggled her fingers. "Now, if you please."

"I can assist you."

Violet released a sigh of frustration. Her eyes might have rolled toward the sky, too. "That is hardly necessary."

"What if I insisted?"

Curiosity made her ask, "Why are you pursuing this course?"

His brow furrowed. "Pursuing what course?"

"Holding my books hostage with your gallantry," she exclaimed in an unladylike burst.

Movement played about his mouth. Was he— Was the dratted man holding back a smile?

Perhaps she did appear a trifle silly. At last, she relented, seeing no other option. "I have one more call to make."

"Then let us proceed."

"But what about your horse?" She looked about for the animal and found him being tended by a lad of early teen years.

"I handed him off to Timmy, the stable lad at the inn."

Only then, Violet realized this whole kerfuffle had occurred in front of the Queen's Arms, the village's lone inn and tavern, and in full view of anyone and everyone who happened past. "Follow me." She set out at a brisk clip as she crossed the street that had given her so much trouble minutes ago.

A chuckle sounded at her back. "Might we walk beside one another?"

Unwillingly, Violet slowed her pace. In truth, she felt the sting of foolishness, but was having trouble correcting the behavior. "Of course," she ground out.

In silence, they walked side by side, not touching, not speaking. She should have informed Sinclair that it went against all that was proper that he—an eligible gentleman—escort her—a marriageable miss—anywhere, for she'd set out today without a female companion or servant. The longer she remained unmarried, the more lax Mama and Papa were about such matters. Of course, she'd had no way of predicting that Will Sinclair would appear from nowhere and insist on playing the gallant.

Still, she was Violet Hotchkiss. In a few years, she would be an outright spinster, and everyone knew it. Her reputation was safe.

Her final delivery of the day would have been a quick call—as little Janie Timpkins knew exactly the books she wanted—were it not for Mrs. Timpkins. When she noticed it was Mr. Will Sinclair accompanying Violet, the woman had insisted on serving them a spot of tea. In all the months she'd been delivering books to the Timpkins household, Violet had never been offered a dram of tea or refreshment of any sort. Not once. Instead, Mrs. Timpkins mostly grumbled about the necessity of reading for a girl, to which Violet invariably responded, "But she could find occupation in the General Post Office like your cousin Nancy, but only if she knows her letters." The argument silenced Mrs. Timpkins every time.

Today, however, no such grumblings sounded. Today, Mrs. Timpkins was serving tea and refreshment to the son of Sir John Sinclair. But Violet had a feeling it wasn't that fact that was brightening the woman's cheek with a rosy blush. With his sharp cheekbones, deep-set blue eyes, straight nose, strong jaw, and dimpled chin, Will Sinclair was simply impossibly handsome, a fact too apparent not to notice.

Except, Sinclair himself seemed not to give it any thought, which, admittedly, was a rare quality in an exceptional looking person. Somehow, it only enhanced his attractiveness, even as it served to put others at their ease. From her place across the room with Janie, Violet could see it worked on Mrs. Timpkins as he inquired about her day and listened as she spoke, his head cocked with interest.

Until today, Violet had never noticed this about Sinclair, his ability to draw people out and truly hear them. Someday, when he took over Somerton Manor, he would make an exceedingly good and capable landowner.

Not that it was any of Violet's concern.

Janie finished picking her two books for the week, and Violet began restacking the rest she would carry home. They were quite a load, if she was being honest. Before she could pick up the stack, Sinclair was beside her. "If I may?"

Violet contained an impatient huff, even as she stood back. It didn't do any good to argue with the man. "Of course."

Within a few minutes, they'd spoken their farewells to a beaming Mrs. Timpkins and were walking up the narrow lane back to the high street, again side by side, again silent. Violet couldn't understand if Sinclair put most people at ease, why did he set her so on edge?

She might have to consider the fault lay entirely with her, including her present rudeness by not speaking to him. She cleared her throat. "About your travels," she began. "How is it you were gone for over three years? I remember it bandied about that you would be gone for a year or two."

"Well, Napoleon had just finished laying waste to Europe when I got over to France, so travel was slow as I continued on to Italy. The idea was a Grand Tour sort of journey. You know, the Renaissance and Classics. It was down through Florence and Rome, then up to Venice. Next thing, I found myself in Greece." He emitted a chuckle from deep inside his chest. "And on it went until I woke up one day in Constantinople. I was like a feather in the wind for a time."

Although Violet had had no intention of being charmed by him—after all, she'd only set out to be *not* rude—she couldn't help being so. The idea of being a feather in the wind called to a wild place in her that had never been fully tamed. "I've only experienced such a life in books."

He cast a sharp eye in her direction. "You have a desire to see the world?"

Violet gave a short laugh that couldn't help being self-conscious. "I think I might. I've heard that Florence is a city of much beauty. And, supposedly, Michelangelo's statue of David must be seen to be believed."

A smile tipped at the side of Sinclair's mouth. "His state of undress wouldn't be of bother to you?"

A blush heated Violet's cheeks. "The human body is a thing of nature. Why should it?" she asked with more bravery than she felt. "But books will have to do," she finished on a bright chirp that rang false. "And now you're returned."

He nodded. "I am."

Even though this was possibly the longest conversation she'd ever held with Will Sinclair, Violet detected a tone. Mayhap his own wistfulness. "Do you wish you were still on your travels?"

Why had she asked such a very personal question? Because she was curious, that was why. Nothing got between Violet and her curiosity, not even propriety.

"Not particularly. It was time to return home." He hesitated. "And assume my place."

Immediately, Violet understood. Sinclair was Sir John's only son. As such, he had responsibilities and duties. *Here.* Not in exotic corners of the globe.

They turned onto the high street and a figure caught Violet's eye. Mr. Oliver Quincy, not twenty feet away, standing on the door-step of a shop while he tipped his beaver hat to just the correct angle. Her heart gave a lurch in her chest and skipped a few beats. The man was so refined and elegant.

And so completely opposite the man beside her.

She experienced a pang at the observation. Was that guilt?

"Quincy," called Sinclair, gaining the man's attention.

A dignified smile on his face, Mr. Quincy began to amble toward them. A wave of heat flushed through Violet, and she had a strong suspicion twin patches of bright pink now adorned her cheeks.

And the smile that pulled at every muscle in her face? Well, she couldn't control that either. In truth, she'd never felt herself smile so, but there seemed to be no help for it.

Every ideal the perfect hero would possess, Mr. Quincy embodied.

Only with great mental fortitude did Will suppress the snort that wanted release at the way Violet Hotchkiss was gazing upon Quincy.

So, too, did he have to tamp down a violent surge of envy. She'd never once regarded him in such a manner, which bordered on the worshipful. "What brings you out, Quincy?" he asked, unable to keep the gruffness out of his voice.

Not that the ever self-involved Quincy would notice. Instead, the man glanced meaningfully down at the pile of books in Will's arms. "I could ask the same of you, old chap."

Miss Hotchkiss gave a laugh that trilled across the breeze. What a light, lovely laugh.

For Quincy.

Right.

"Mr. Sinclair is carrying my circulating children's library," she explained.

"Ah, you don't say," Quincy said, sounding thoroughly disinterested, which Miss Hotchkiss didn't seem to notice.

"Yes, today is Tuesday," she said.

"Indeed, it is."

Quincy hadn't caught the import of Miss Hotchkiss's remark. Will had to resist the urge to cuff the man about the ears.

"We discussed it last night," she continued, undeterred.

"Oh, yes, well, then. There you have it," Quincy concluded rather vacuously.

Quincy sounded utterly dismissive and patronizing toward Miss Hotchkiss, but her bright, smitten expression indicated she didn't notice.

And Will had always thought her so sensible.

"Are you in our neighborhood for long, Mr. Quincy?" she asked, shyly.

"In fact, I am considering a property about five miles to the east."

"Oh?"

That breathy *"Oh"* made her sound entirely too interested in the future whereabouts of Oliver Quincy.

"Since Father passed away, Mamma has wanted to be closer to her sister." Quincy didn't need anyone's input to carry on a conversation.

"What a tender heart you have, Mr. Quincy, to perform such a duty for your mother."

Oliver Quincy? Tender hearted? Like the conceited nitwit he was, Quincy beamed at the praise.

Will might be sick. More like the man wanted to get his mother out of their London townhouse and out to pasture in the country.

"During all the talk about the Earl and Countess of Holland's Twelfth Night Ball," Miss Hotchkiss said, "I do not remember hearing if you will be in attendance."

Rather bold of Miss Hotchkiss, but Will shouldn't have been surprised. She had always been one to pursue her interests with a dogged resoluteness.

"Indeed, I shall," Quincy stated in a tone which implied his very presence would be doing the Earl and Countess a favor. "The Countess and Mamma debuted the same year and have been bosom friends since."

"Oh, how very fortuitous," Miss Hotchkiss all but exclaimed with delight.

Will could no longer abide the way she was gazing upon Quincy, who took her drooling appreciation of him as his God-given right. As Quincy did with everything in life, always had.

If Miss Hotchkiss ever were to gaze upon him that way, well, Will might ask her to marry him on the spot.

But she wasn't.

So, he wouldn't.

Right.

Will looked up to find the Queen's Arms sign swinging above them, the inn where he'd left his horse and where he would leave Quincy to Miss Hotchkiss. Best of luck to her. The thought had him feeling immensely grumpy.

"Quincy, if you will take these..." Will held out the children's books.

Eyes wide with surprise, Quincy held up his hands. "What is this, old chap?"

"I have a meeting with Father's steward, and I'll be late if I do not depart now." It was only the truth. "You, cousin, need to carry these for Miss Hotchkiss."

"You will have noticed I made a purchase at the mercantile." Quincy held up a thin parcel wrapped in brown paper and twine. Possibly, it weighed less than the lightest of the children's books.

Miss Hotchkiss, however, didn't seem to notice how ungentlemanly and self-centered Quincy was. "I carry these books every Tuesday." She was already extending her arms to take the load. "Truly, there is no need."

Will wasn't sure with whom he was more frustrated, Quincy or Miss Hotchkiss. Mayhap they were perfect for each other. Still, he couldn't simply leave it. He shoved the books toward Quincy. "Can you, at least, hold them while I mount?"

Once on his horse, Will reached down and took the unwieldy pile from Quincy, even as he addressed his next words to Miss Hotchkiss. "I shall deliver these to your house on my way."

"Sinclair, that is quite unnecessary, I can assure you," she protested. "I have been making these deliveries every Tuesday for the last two years."

Will glanced down at the pair of patronizing smiles

staring up at him. Had the world gone wrong side up? Since when was it ridiculous to be a gentleman? So he wouldn't shout at the two of them, Will, instead, tipped his hat to Miss Hotchkiss. "I bid you a good day."

With that, Will urged his horse to a canter down the High Street. A trill of laughter might have sounded at his back.

Frustrating woman.

Stupid man.

Perhaps they deserved each other. Except...

Will couldn't help thinking that Violet Hotchkiss deserved better.

Chapter Four

One might not suppose the heart of a bespectacled, confirmed bluestocking—some in this magnificent ballroom might even whisper a *spinster* —to brim over with joy at a ball, but Violet's always had.

It was true that she didn't dance as much as other young ladies and that her dance card accrued fewer names with each year that had passed since her come-out. But those trivialities could never interfere with her enjoyment of a ball, particularly one as splendid as the Earl and Countess of Holland's annual Twelfth Night Ball at Welles Castle. Composed of mellow golden-hued stone, it was a grand country house whose very sight was enough to proclaim its importance to the world, with its wide, imposing colonnade at the front entrance and ornamental turrets flanking either side in perfect symmetry.

Every year, it was the light that first overwhelmed her when she entered the ballroom, as overhead, multi-tiered, crystal chandeliers dropped from ornate ceiling roses, receiving brilliant candlelight and throwing it about in a hundred sparkling directions. Mahogany floors below gleamed a rich red with the light and reflected it with a mirror shine. Ladies' bare shoulders and décolletage glowed cream with it, and gentlemen's shirtfronts stark, fresh white. Vibrancy glittered through trilling laughter and incautious smiles and sparked the air alive, combining to form an atmosphere of life lived in its most giddy state.

How she loved to soak it in, her toes tapping beneath her dress, the blood effervescing through her veins. If this ballroom were a glass, its occupants would be the champagne, their laughter and delight fizzing up its glittering walls. This was where life was truly lived, inside this joy.

Of course, the fact that she had danced the opening set with Mr. Quincy might have something to do with this feeling shimmering through Violet. It was the most perfect set she had ever danced. Truly, she should have known Mr. Quincy, with his thin, elegant form, would excel at dancing, as surely he did in every other aspect of his life.

Simply look at him now, dancing with yet another partner. He hadn't skipped a single set, as was his duty as an eligible, single gentleman. He must be exhausted. But the fact that he had singled her out for the first set spoke all the volumes Violet needed to hear.

Still, it wasn't as if she had been sitting with the other wallflowers this entire time. In fact, she had danced sets with two other gentlemen and strolled the room with Lily, who was now laughing at some quip her dance partner had just made.

A throat cleared at her side, and Violet's head whipped around, a happy smile curled about her mouth. *Will Sinclair.* Her smile fell. She'd been so entirely concentrated upon Mr. Quincy, she hadn't noticed Sinclair's approach.

"Would you care to dance a set with me?"

"I, uh—" She had never been so unprepared for a question in all her life. She dug inside her reticule and pulled out her dance card. It was almost entirely devoid of names. But he didn't have to know that. "It will be a few hours, I'm afraid."

Sinclair's eyebrows lifted in disbelief. "As you may have noticed, a new set is beginning, and you do not appear to have a dance partner."

Heat flushed through Violet. He had her there, his eyes told her. They also told her that he wasn't inclined to leave anytime soon. And she needed to rid herself of him. She'd lost track of Mr. Quincy on the dancing floor. "I am parched," burst out from her the instant the happy lie came to her. "Would you, perhaps, fetch me a glass of punch?"

Those deep blue eyes of Sinclair's narrowed slightly, and she thought he might refuse her request. But, after an interminable three seconds, he nodded, pivoted on his heel, and strode away on the errand.

Relief soared through Violet, even as her gaze began a desperate search of the room, lighting through the gay crowd—the sparkling laughter, the glittering tiaras, the rustling silks, the flirtatious rap of a closed fan, a couple wed only today staring so deeply into one another's eyes, one had to glance away—when, at last, she spotted Mr. Quincy. He stood, alone, at the edge of the crowd. Brow crinkled and intent, he, too, was surveying the ballroom.

Then his eye caught on Violet's. It was hardly for the flash of a second, but long enough to set her heart racing. She only noticed he was near an exterior door when he stepped back, cracked it open, and disappeared outside.

Violet's heart lurched into a full gallop. What had just happened? Had she been summoned for a secret rendezvous?

Her ever logical mind quickly retraced the order of events. She had been scanning the ballroom. Mr. Quincy had been scanning the ballroom. His eye met hers. Then he slipped through the outside door.

What gave her pause, however, was the length of time their eyes met. It had been a fleeting contact, undeniably. But... wasn't that the way of discretion?

Again, her mind raced through the logic. This was a ball. Secret assignations occurred at balls.

Well, not to her.

Not... until tonight?

Violet's mouth went dry, and her feet started moving. As she pushed the exterior door open, a blast of wintry air greeted her full in the face, but it gave her no pause as her eyes cast about for Mr. Quincy. She detected not a sign of him on the terrace.

On quick feet, she took the stone staircase that led down into the garden. It was new moon dark, but the chandelier light that poured from the house and the sporadically hung globe lanterns scattered throughout the shrubberies enveloped the garden within an otherworldly spell. She wouldn't be at all surprised to learn that fairies frolicked here every Twelfth Night. Its magic swept her up, slowing her pace along the garden path, the light crunch of gravel beneath her feet.

She rounded a shrubby corner and, at last, found

Mr. Quincy. His back to her some distance away, he stood alone.

He was waiting.

For *her*.

Violet opened her mouth to call his name and stopped herself. Other ears might be milling about, and it wouldn't do to attract their attention. After all, she was a respectable young lady. Instead, she stalked slowly forward, an indiscreet smile on her lips, an incautious joy in her heart.

Movement beyond Mr. Quincy's shoulder stopped Violet in her tracks as the figure of a young lady appeared in the clearing. Violet's smile faltered. The young lady, too, was wearing a smile, the same indiscreet one that had curled about Violet's mouth but a moment ago.

As if time slowed its tick-tock, Violet watched in budding horror while the young lady rushed toward Mr. Quincy. If Violet had been harboring any doubts as to the scene before her, they were erased when Mr. Quincy's arms opened and took the young lady into his embrace.

Violet's hand flew to her mouth, muffling her gasp, and hot tears flooded her eyes as the truth walloped her. Mr. Quincy had been making a secret assignation.

But not with her.

She'd had it all wrong.

Oh, that a hole would open in the ground and swallow her up.

Then she remembered her pride. She must flee before they caught her staring and matters became even worse.

Violet's feet kicked into motion, and she ran. Soon, however, she realized that instead of returning to the house, she'd fled in the opposite direction.

The tears she had been holding back finally fell. Tears of hurt. Tears of stupidity. But, mostly, tears of humiliation.

She gave her eyes a hard swipe and, unthinking, knocked the spectacles from her face. "Oh, bollocks!" she cried, squinting at the ground, but the combination of the night's darkness and her nearsightedness made it impossible to see.

Frantic, she crashed down to her knees to search with her hands, but to no avail. More tears sprang to her eyes, and she collapsed on her backside with an unlady-like thud. These tears, however, were of frustration as the enormity of her mistake sank in, followed swiftly by a clearing dose of reality.

Mr. Quincy had only danced with her first to get their set out of the way.

Mr. Quincy had only ever been polite to her.

Mr. Quincy was never going to meet her for a secret rendezvous, because he saw her for who she truly was, a bespectacled, bluestocking future spinster.

She would never have a secret rendezvous. She would never have a kiss stolen in the dark to the distant strings of a mazurka. She would never be seen the way Mr. Quincy saw that other young lady.

Violet inhaled a wretched sob. The next instant, feeling the ridiculousness of her situation, she exhaled a wobbly laugh. At least no one was here to witness her humiliation.

"Miss Hotchkiss?" came a deep, masculine voice.

She went utterly still.

"Miss Hotchkiss?"

Her eyes squinched shut. *No.* It couldn't be.

"Miss Hotchkiss?"

It could be, and it was.

From her seated position, she twisted around. *Sinclair.* Still too tall, too massive, and, presumably, too handsome, though she couldn't see his face as his back was to the dim light that only just reached from the ballroom. What in the blazes was he doing here?

"Are you injured?" he asked, his voice ripe with concern.

Violet heaved a deep, shaky sigh. "I've—" She held up empty, helpless hands. "Oh, I've lost my spectacles."

"May I help you search for them?"

"Oh, why bother? I'm fairly certain I heard them hit a stone. They are likely cracked." She sounded pathetic to her own ears. She could only imagine how she sounded to Sinclair.

But it mattered not, for the next moment, he was crouched beside her, scouring the ground. "They are here, somewhere." He sounded very focused.

In the face of his sudden intensity, Violet said nothing more. She simply sat while he searched for several minutes. The man was stubborn. Until recently, she hadn't known that about him.

"Ah," he said. Violet detected triumph in the syllable. "Here they are."

Sinclair sprang to his feet and stepped close enough for Violet to take them. Gingerly, she attempted to perch them on her nose, but one lens was cracked and the frame had twisted, so they sat lopsided. In short, the spectacles were a mangled mess, but she felt oddly touched by Sinclair's dogged pursuit and recovery of them. She wouldn't have expected it of him. She'd cast Mr. Quincy as the ideal hero and Sinclair as the rake. Mayhap she would have to reassess that conclusion.

He offered his hand. "May I assist you to your feet?"

Violet's first instinct was to refuse. Then she realized he wasn't truly asking. His hand was extended, implacable. She must accept his help. She placed her hand in his, and, through the satin of her gloves, she felt his warmth and strength as he pulled her to her feet without effort.

But it wasn't that sensation which sent the blood fizzing through her veins. It was the very *male* feel of him. In all their childhood spent in proximity to one another, she had never once touched Sinclair. She would have remembered this feeling, this response.

"Can you see without them?" he asked.

"Not very well," she confessed.

But she didn't need spectacles to see what was becoming crystal clear to her. This feel of Sinclair... his strength, his masculinity... Had she always suspected it, and therefore shied away from him?

Will Sinclair had ever overwhelmed her, from the first moment she'd met him when she'd been a girl and he a boy. This moment was no different.

Except it was.

She glanced down at his large hand wrapped around her smaller one. The descriptor for him, the one that hovered just out of reach when she thought of the newly returned Will Sinclair, came to her. *Experienced.*

Sinclair had returned to their quaint neighborhood an experienced man. And that experience suited her needs perfectly at the moment, even as it made her quake in her slippers.

His brow furrowed. "Is there something more I can do for you?" he asked, the question a velvety rumble that inspired a melting sensation inside Violet.

She gave her bottom lip a nervous lick. Sinclair's eye followed the motion, sending a frisson of anticipation through her. "Yes."

The fact was she didn't have to miss out on everything a young lady enjoyed. She could, in fact, take a bit of life's wild, indiscreet joy for herself.

An expectant air hung about him as he waited for her to continue. Her heart raced. Could she speak the words suspended on the tip of her tongue?

If she didn't, what then? What would she have gained?

What would she have lost?

Violet stiffened her spine and met Sinclair's questioning eye. "Kiss me."

Will blinked.

"*Kiss* you?" He had to ask.

Miss Hotchkiss blinked her wide violet eyes. "Unless," she began.

Was that a wobble in her voice? Will was helpless against a wobble in a woman's voice.

"Unless you wouldn't care to."

"Unless I wouldn't…"

She inhaled a deep, shaky breath. "I am, after all," she said, "a bespectacled future spinster." She swallowed. "And you are the most handsome man in any room."

Somewhere between an inhale and an exhale, the breath froze in Will's chest, her words catching him on his heels. They didn't sound like a compliment. Had he, in fact, just been insulted?

When Miss Hotchkiss opened her mouth to keep talking, Will did the only thing that could possibly shut her up. He angled his face down and pressed his mouth to hers. Her eyes went wide for a shocked instant. Then she sighed a little groan, and he caught it in his mouth.

He reached for the small of her back, and she swayed forward, erasing the distance between them, her lithe body up against him, his cock throbbing to life in response. Her hands found the nape of his neck, her nails a light scrape against his skin, fine hairs prickling with goose bumps. The kiss had no choice but to deepen as his tongue slid along her plump lower lip. She gave a tiny gasp. But shock quickly became curiosity as her tongue poked forward, then tangled with his.

How many times had he imagined taking Miss Hotchkiss in his arms? Of kissing her? Her sway, her surrender... The feel of her lissome body, the taste of her pert mouth. *Spiced pear.*

He felt hot and alive, and he wanted more.

He wanted everything.

But... she hadn't asked for more.

And certainly not for everything.

With a resoluteness Will hadn't known he possessed, he pulled away and broke the kiss. Surprise traced through Miss Hotchkiss's glazed eyes, and her breath puffed white through the upturned "O" of her kiss-crushed lips. It was all Will could do not to pull her into him and claim them again.

He was opening his mouth to offer her an apology—although for what precisely he wasn't exactly sure since she'd asked for the kiss, except it was the gentlemanly thing to do—when a snowflake fluttered through the air and landed on the tip of her nose. Then fell another, which tangled in her eyelashes. She blinked the snowflake away and breathed out a little laugh as her head tipped back to take in the light snowfall swirling about them, an awed smile curved about her mouth.

Oh, Violet Hotchkiss was a temptation.

Perhaps he could tempt her again.

Then her gaze returned to him, and her smile fell by

slow increments. A seriousness formed about her, and her head tipped to the side, a tendency of Miss Hotchkiss's since childhood. She was about to ask a question, most likely one that would make its recipient uncomfortable. He braced himself.

"Did you follow me, Sinclair?"

Will would have to tread carefully. "When I was returning with your punch—"

"You retrieved the punch?"

"Of course. You asked for it. Anyway, I noticed you leaving the ballroom."

"And?"

"You weren't wearing a cloak."

"So, you followed me?"

"I thought you might be cold." It was only the truth.

Miss Hotchkiss touched delicate fingertips to her mouth and shifted a step back. Every cell in Will's body screamed *no*.

"I kissed you," she said with no small amount of amazement, as if only now realizing it.

"I believe it was mutual."

"I've been kissed."

"I believe that fact has been fairly established."

"I've been kissed by"—her eyes went wide—"*you*."

For the second time in the last five minutes, Will

wasn't sure he'd received a compliment. "Was there someone else you expected to kiss tonight?"

A wince passed across her face, and Will knew. Indeed, Violet Hotchkiss had expected to be kissed tonight.

By another man.

Before Will could press the matter further, two figures emerged from behind a distant hedgerow. It was a young lady and... *Right.*

Will understood exactly who Miss Hotchkiss expected to kiss.

Quincy.

Of course. She was besotted with the dolt. Will could growl with frustration.

The other couple turned the opposite direction and hastened toward the house, without noticing their observers. Miss Hotchkiss exhaled a rough breath, shaky and shivery.

Without a staying thought, Will shed his tailcoat and had the garment draped across her shoulders before she could refuse it. He liked her wearing his coat, even though she swam in it.

"I do not need this." She shivered again.

"You do."

"I must return to the ballroom. My sister will be wondering where I am."

"After you."

"You do not need to keep following me," she huffed, pettish.

No matter. He waved his arm forward, this time wordlessly signaling, "After you."

With an easy stride, Will followed Miss Hotchkiss, whose shorter legs were moving at a near jog. This night had certainly taken a turn. He'd even considered not attending the ball, certain he would be subjected to watching Violet Hotchkiss moon over Quincy all night. But the lure of dancing a set with her had been too great a temptation to resist. In all the years of their acquaintance, and all the fêtes and assemblies they had attended, he'd never once success-fully asked her to dance. She'd always managed to elude him somehow. Tonight, he'd meant to set that situation to rights.

And then, of all things, she'd pleaded with him to kiss her.

He gave his head a confounded shake. The first of many, he was certain.

As they neared the stone staircase that led up to the terrace, the happy strains of violin and cello ribboned through the air. Light shone through ballroom windows, illuminating dancers intent on their scandalous waltz. Miss Hotchkiss stopped and shrugged off the coat.

"Keep it," Will said instinctively.

She heaved a longsuffering sigh. "Sinclair, I can*not* enter that room wearing your tailcoat. I would be ruined."

"Not if you married me."

What the blazes had he just said?

Violet gave a laugh bursting with disbelief. "We both know that isn't happening."

"Would it be the worst thing?" he asked on a low rumble. For whatever reason, he was piqued by her response.

A trio of shocked seconds ticked past before another laugh startled from her. "I think you and I both know the answer to that question."

Without another word, Miss Hotchkiss handed the coat over and nimbly ascended the steps. Will didn't take his eyes off her until she disappeared into the ballroom. For his part, he wasn't going back in there. He couldn't and keep his hands off her. The two possibilities didn't exist in the same space together.

"I think you and I both know the answer to that question."

She might know the answer, but did he?

He couldn't be sure their answers would align with one another. Yet another reason he wouldn't return to that ballroom. He might demand *her* answer.

And, really, what right had he to make demands of her? It was only a kiss that had occurred between them.

If only that were true.

Will shrugged on his coat and caught a wisp of her scent of roses. On his next inhalation, it was gone. He experienced a fleeting pang of loss.

He would have to leave Violet Hotchkiss be; that was the truth of it. The kiss that had occurred between them was an anomaly. She hadn't truly wanted him. She'd wanted Quincy. Will had been naught more than a substitute. Bitter thought.

He dug hands deep into his pockets, hoping to fight off the chill of the night. His fingers touched cold metal. To his surprise, his hand emerged holding Miss Hotchkiss's spectacles. They were completely destroyed. Even so, he should hie after her and return them. Instead, he placed them in his pocket and strode into the night.

On the long walk home, he wouldn't think about the fact that a frisson of joy might have traced through him at the prospect of having a piece of Violet Hotchkiss to himself.

Chapter Five

March

"I am still quite confused as to how you lost the spectacles, Vivi."

"As I have told you." Violet tried not to lose patience with her sister. But, really, it had been two months, and Lily still hadn't let the matter go. Forbearance had its limits. "I was swiping a foreign object from my eyes"—she wouldn't mention the fact that said foreign object was a flood of tears—"and they flew off my face." At least that part was true.

"And you couldn't find them?"

"It was dark." Another truth.

"But what I don't understand is how you were out of doors in the first place."

"I simply opened a door and stepped outside."

Lily huffed. "That pert mouth of yours. Shall I rephrase? *Why* were you outside?"

"I needed fresh air," Violet stated firmly, as if it were the truth and not, instead, a bald-faced lie.

She wouldn't—*couldn't*—relate the humiliating misunderstanding that had led to her being out of doors, not even to Lily.

"Oh, Vivi, only you would seek out fresh air in the midst of a snowstorm."

Violet hadn't been the only one, another detail she wasn't about to disclose to Lily, for from that disclosure it was but a few short admissions until she reached... *the kiss.*

Even two months later, it was never too far from her mind. In fact, all she had to do was close her eyes, and there *he* was, his too handsome face angling toward her, his intense gaze burning for... *her.*

Warmth flooded through her every time she remembered. *Warmth* might be too tame a word for the feeling. *Hot. Incendiary. Scorching.*

Every night, when she closed her eyes to sleep, well, it was a problem.

Ahead, Granville Court slipped into view. It was a pleasing square manor house constructed of stone and red brick in the last century. Lily's talented hand in the garden had lent both the house and surrounding grounds an inviting loveliness that, on a warm summer's day, tempted one to smell the riots of overgrown flowers and lie on the springy green turf and daydream the hours away. So, too, it had the added benefit of being not half a mile away from Hotchkiss House, where Violet still lived with her parents.

On this day, however, Violet thanked the heavens at the sight of it for an altogether different reason. She was ready to deposit her sister and her prying questions at her home.

"Oh! I almost forgot," exclaimed Lily of a sudden. "Have any more Sir Pug books arrived?"

Relieved that Lily had moved on to this less distressing—and heat inducing—subject, Violet smiled. "In fact," she said with no small amount of excitement, "I received another installment last evening."

Lily clapped. "Is it as adorable as *Sir Pug Goes to Town?*"

"Indeed, it is."

"What is it called?" asked Lily, her delight seemingly unable to be contained.

"*Sir Pug Explores the Stables.*"

"You must bring it tomorrow for our walk."

Four weeks ago, Violet had received the first book of the Adventures of Sir Pug, written by an author with whom she was unfamiliar, one E.B. McWoof, a name which was surely a pseudonym. The tales followed the adventures of a jaunty, monocled pug exploring London in a top hat, evening jacket, and cane, and were already a ripping success with the children on her library circuit. And while the stories were simple and cute, it was the illustrations that were particularly delightful. In truth, they were beautifully rendered in pencil and watercolor.

"And you've still no idea who sent them?"

Violet shook her head. "Not a one."

"Well, either the renown of your children's library is growing or..." A mischievous smile curled about Lily's mouth.

Violet knew that smile of her sister's. "*Or?*"

Lily gave her eyebrows a little waggle. "Or you've an admirer."

The very idea squeezed a laugh from Violet. "It's much more likely the former than the latter."

"Oh, Vivi, one day an infatuation is going to wallop you over the head, and you won't know what happened."

Violet averted her gaze. The humiliation of just that was still too fresh, and she wasn't eager to repeat the experience. None of which she would be telling Lily.

Lily gave her belly a rub, which she had taken to doing as it had started expanding. Violet experienced the familiar pang of envy.

"Shall I send for the carriage to drive you home?"

Violet shook her head. "The weather is warming nicely. I shall take advantage of this bit of early spring and extend my walk."

Lily yawned daintily behind her hand. "And I shall nap."

With that, Violet left her sister and continued on. Instead of turning toward home at the end of the drive, she rambled down the lane in the opposite direction. It wasn't long before she encountered a trail veering off the road. On a whim, she took it and found herself winding through woodland verdant with newly emergent spring growth. She inhaled deeply of air fresh and earthy and smiled down to her soul. One's cares had no hold in such an environ. They simply fell away as one succumbed to its peace.

Too soon, she emerged from the woods and found herself at the top of a hill, at its bottom a lazy winding river. She'd wandered onto Sir John's land, she realized. Best not to think of Sir John as it only conjured thoughts of his son, as if the blasted man needed any invitation to enter her head. Best she turn homeward. Except...

As she gazed down the hill sloping away from her, she felt another smile pulling at her, one of unfiltered joy. This was the sort of hill that had ever tempted her childhood self to start running as fast as her feet could carry her. Without conscious command, they started moving, the memory in her body too powerful to deny. Before she knew it, she was racing down the hill, inhaling and exhaling in short sharp bursts, legs and lungs burning with the effort, face painful with what felt like the biggest, most indiscriminate smile of her life.

She reached the bottom, tall grass swaying about her knees, and doubled over, chest heaving as she laughed at her silly, girlish self. Oh, how good it felt.

Cheeks hot and breath puffing white with steam, she straightened, swiped beads of perspiration off her forehead, and took in the view. Across the grass, beyond a small boathouse, flowed the river, smooth and glassy, tall reeds at its banks, green willow trees bent in their familiar, elegant drape. So lovely and peaceful. To bear witness to such a sight made one feel like God's chosen creature.

Movement flickered at the distant bend of the river. Hand to her forehead for shade, she squinted and found a small boat, rowed by a single occupant, gliding across the glassy surface, leaving tiny ripples in its wake. The motion of the oars was rhythmic and assured. Drawn in by the unexpected sight, Violet moved toward the water's edge, her focus fast upon the rower, whose back was to her.

Sinclair.

Recognition only enhanced her fascination. As her

mouth went dry, she might have to accept it only increased the allure. That white linen shirt stuck to his broad back, his muscles bunching in flex and release. Sleeves rolled to his elbows, forearms sinewy and tensile with strain as his torso pitched forward and legs pushed back in perfect sync. Sun glinting golden streaks through his hair, Sinclair was quite simply gorgeous, the stuff of Greek mythology. *Adonis.*

And this Adonis had kissed her.

Until the night of the ball, she had never viewed Sinclair in this light. He was slightly older with a handsomeness so conspicuous and undeniable that it had always been forbidding to her. He'd always been the most handsome boy, and now he was the most handsome man. She had always assumed him destined to marry an equally handsome woman with whom he would beget handsome children, and she'd left it at that. These conclusions had always kept him at a safe remove from her.

But now she couldn't quite achieve the old distance. He was so very alive, and so very much a *man* with his muscles and sweat, that he felt immediate to her. She knew the press of his mouth, the scent of his skin, the feel of those long, masculine fingers that were presently wrapped around the oars.

Perspiration pinpricked Violet's skin, and it wasn't

from sun or exertion. If she was being honest with herself, this new feeling was the true reason why she'd avoided all social functions that might include Sinclair these last few months. She couldn't gaze upon him and *not* think of him this way.

And it wasn't simply the fact that he was an Adonis. Will Sinclair was interesting and shockingly easy to like. He had traveled, and he read novels. In the garden at the Twelfth Night Ball, she'd discovered he was kind. Above all else, she might like this best about him.

Now, she couldn't help viewing him in a light that revealed more than his male beauty, but also, somehow, the truth of him. Ever since the night of the ball.

A mortified groan escaped her. She'd been such a ninny that night over Mr. Quincy. She should have known—she *did* know—that she wasn't the sort of woman who men lost their heads over. She would never marry. She would never again experience the sort of kiss Sinclair had laid upon her.

She attempted to feel matter-of-fact about it. She'd all but begged him. So, he'd done it to be polite. What choice had he as a gentleman?

In truth, that thought made her feel a little despairing.

With each stroke of the oar, her heart inserted an extra beat into its rhythm as he drew nearer. Soon, he shot past her on smooth water. From beneath the determined furrow of his brow, his gaze lifted and met hers. His eyes went wide with surprise before he pushed his oars in the opposing direction, thereby halting the momentum of the skiff. The moment stretched long as his gaze silently held hers across the short distance. His skin flush with exertion, a bead of sweat trickled down the side of his face.

And Violet thought it wasn't possible for him to be more attractive. She had been wrong.

In that instant, she knew. She wanted something more from this man than his kiss. Something proper young ladies didn't think about until their wedding night.

But she wasn't so young anymore.

And she wouldn't be having a wedding night.

But neither fact meant she couldn't have this man.

She stopped herself right there. Could she be considering what she thought she might be considering?

She was.

She needed to turn around and run back up that hill like the devil was at her back.

He was.

As if by the sheer strength of his thoughts Will could make her materialize, there, on the river bank, stood Violet Hotchkiss—*Violet*, as his mind insisted on thinking of her—dressed in a white muslin morning dress and a Venice blue woolen pelisse to stave off the chill on this morning that wasn't quite cold but not warm either. She looked a treat, even with that curious scowl on her face.

He supposed he should say something. "I see you've obtained new spectacles."

Violet reflexively pushed them up the bridge of her nose. "I am still adjusting to their fit."

The moment grew as awkward as the conversation, but Will had no choice but to keep on with it. "You don't care for them?" He did feel a twinge of guilt at having kept her other pair, but not enough to give them back.

"Not particularly. But the others disappeared that —" Her mouth snapped shut, leaving the last word hanging in the air between them, unspoken. *Night.* And they both knew which night. Body poised on the edge of flight, she said, "I should be—"

"Don't go," Will spoke without thought.

Violet's brow crinkled in its familiar little furrow. He'd always thought it an expression worthy of adoration.

Will pulled the oars into sudden motion and gave

the skiff a great row, banking it on a clear stretch of river shore. He jumped off the bow and landed on marshy grass. "Do you walk this way often?"

"Never." She shifted on her feet. "Well, today."

"May I continue your walk with you?"

"You know that won't do." A laugh escaped her. He detected a hardness within it. "Even for a spinster like me."

This was the second time he'd heard her allude to being a spinster. He didn't care for it. "You? A spinster? I hardly think you're of an age to be making such proclamations."

"A future spinster," she amended.

"I can, at least, walk you to the edge of my family's lands without creating too much of a scandal."

Violet gave a little shrug. Will took that as acceptance.

Silently, and without touching, they took the grassy hill at an easy stride beneath a blue sky dotted with puffy white clouds. A light breeze fluttered through the tall grass and soughed through the trees ahead. With each step, an ease expanded between them.

"Were you rowing for any particular purpose?"

Will shook his head. "I took it up at Oxford. I enjoy the feel of it in my muscles."

Another laugh escaped Violet. This one, Will liked,

for its spontaneity and softness. "I've never once in my life heard a gentleman speak about his muscles."

He'd surprised her. He would enjoy doing it again. "Mayhap I'm not like other gentlemen."

Violet darted a quick glance at him, a serious light in her eyes. "I think, mayhap, you're not."

He detected a change in the way she was regarding him. He might even feel disconcerted by it, but he couldn't help feeling intrigued. Violet Hotchkiss had always been dismissive of him, and now she was... interested?

Again in silence, they walked on, topping the hill and entering the woodland, the canopy above creating an atmosphere of quiet and protection, sunlight dappling through. They could be the only two people in the world.

Will rather liked the thought of that.

Rather too much.

"Might I make a personal inquiry?" Violet asked.

"Certainly."

"Do you plan to stay in the neighborhood?"

"I do."

"No more jaunting about the globe?"

"I believe the travel lust has run its course."

"And what about plans to start a family? Will that be soon?"

Shock traced through Will. "Your question seems to have turned into an inquisition."

"I never was any good at couching my curiosity in a ladylike manner. That was more of Lily's strength."

In truth, this was something Will had always rather appreciated about Violet Hotchkiss, her forthrightness. "To answer your question, I do have plans to start a family."

Violet nodded, distraction in her manner, as if she was chewing on this information and carefully considering her next words. At last, she spoke. "And do you have someone specific in mind with whom you're hoping to proceed with those plans?"

Will exhaled a gusty laugh. The woman had robbed him of speech. The only people who ever asked him such questions were his parents—well, and Mrs. Acton at Father's New Year's evening soirée—but even they beat about the bush with a bit more delicacy. Violet could be so very direct.

Will came to a stop and waited for her to notice. When she finally did and turned, he met her eye and held it captive. He wanted to see her response when he spoke his next words. "I have an idea of one such young lady."

If she asked who, he decided he might just tell her, consequences be damned.

"But you haven't an understanding with her?" she asked.

"No," he stated, his voice pitched low enough that the sound could only be heard by him and her.

Her eyes searching his, she gave another of her silent, ruminating nods—Will was learning to be wary of that nod—and pivoted away from him, her feet on the move again. Soon, they reached the edge of the woods, which was the end of his father's lands in this direction.

Violet stopped and faced Will. "I thank you for your escort, but this is where we must part ways."

Will gave a shallow, gallant bow. "It was my pleasure."

The moment stretched long as neither of them moved to leave. He could take her in his arms. They were that close and that alone. His hands all but begged to be filled with her.

"We shall be seeing each other again," she said.

The statement emerged with an intensity that surprised Will. "I don't doubt it," he said, slowly.

"Soon."

Then Violet whirled in a soft swish of skirts and strode away. Or as much as a lady could stride while wearing a morning gown.

Why did Will feel this sense of foreboding at the prospect of an outcome he would enjoy? For he would like to see her again, *soon*. Very much. Yet... she'd sounded oddly ominous.

What did she have planned next?

A whistle on his lips as he ambled through the woods and toward the river, Will decided he looked forward to finding out.

Chapter Six

Night

Even in fallen night, Will knew every straight and curve of the gravel path that led from Somerton's manor house to the estate's two-hundred-year-old cottage. It had been a long afternoon with his father's steward, Mr. Garth. But this was what it took to learn all aspects of the estate, and Will had committed himself to it.

Amber light shone softly through the cottage's drawing room curtains. Likely the maid had left a lamp burning. Giving it no further thought, he stepped into the front entryway and was just removing his kidskin gloves when movement caught his eye. His head whipped around, and he stopped dead.

Across the room sat Violet Hotchkiss on the sofa before the fire. Time slowed, even as his senses fired up, while her hands busily restacked the large sheets of paper on the low table before her.

Blast. He never showed those to anyone.

"This is unexpected," he said in as neutral a voice as he could muster.

She gave a little laugh, her bright eyes steady upon him, but she said nothing. When she'd told him she would see him soon, it hadn't occurred to him that *soon* meant tonight. "To what do I owe this pleasure?" he asked carefully.

She sank into the cushions at her back and waved a slender hand. "This is a lovely cottage."

She'd avoided his question, and Will was content to let her. He supposed she would state her purpose soon enough. "I requested to occupy it when I returned."

She nodded, understanding in her eyes. "I'd heard. I imagine it wouldn't be easy to return to your parents' roof after three years away."

"No, not so easy."

"And these?" She tapped the stack of papers before her. "Did you collect these on your journeys?"

Will shifted his stance. "Not exactly."

Her head canted. "Are they by a local artist?"

Will grew more uncomfortable by the second. "Of a sort."

Her brow furrowed. "You're not making any—" Her

brow released, the realization plain on her face. "*You* sketched and painted these."

Will tried not to shuffle and failed. All the nervous energy flowing through him had to go somewhere. He must reply. "I did."

She began thumbing through the stack, carefully attentive to each page. Will busied himself by winding his pocket watch. He would rather chew broken glass than watch her judge his work.

"They are so... so," she began.

He braced himself. He couldn't help it.

"*Good.*"

His gaze swung around to meet hers. Every muscle in his body released with relief, even as his heart galloped in his chest. Her praise entered him with a disconcerting ease, as if he'd been waiting for it all his life.

"The detail—" She went on scanning the pages, oblivious to her effect on him. "The artistry. The precision." She held up one watercolor and viewed it from different angles. "This flower is so lifelike. It's as if I'm holding it in my hands."

Will could see she wouldn't let this go on her own, and as much he couldn't help soaking it in, her praise sat within him at an uncomfortable angle. He murmured a "Thank you, Miss Hotchkiss," but she kept on.

"Yours is no common talent, Sinclair. You could publish these for botanical study."

Will gave a short laugh. "That is the furthest from my intentions."

Her gaze, quizzical and intense, lifted and met his. "Why ever not?"

"'Tis something I do to fill my idle time."

Her eyes narrowed, and she shook her head slowly. "I do not believe you."

As if she'd ever taken the time to know him, he could say and move the conversation in a different direction. But she was correct not to believe him, for it wasn't the full truth. "It was explained to me long ago in no uncertain terms that I have other duties in life."

Sudden understanding shone in her eyes. "The estate."

"I am the only son."

"But—"

It was a fact that she was tenacious as a terrier once she got an idea in her head. He wished she would let it be. Yet so, too, did he want to hear what she had to say. Generally speaking, Violet Hotchkiss voiced opinions and views worth hearing. "*But?*"

"But why can't you be more than one thing? Why can't you be both a country gentleman and an artist?"

She gave the stack of watercolors an emphatic tap. "You are that good."

Her appreciation spread through him like a ray of sun peeking out from behind a cloud on a winter's day. It was a warmth he hadn't known he needed until it streamed into him. He must leave off this subject, fast. Otherwise, he would sink into it and let her keep warming him with praise.

"Miss Hotchkiss," he began formally. Formality seemed the best course. "I suppose you will be telling me your purpose in coming here tonight?"

Even from across the room, he noticed her body lock in tension. Discomfort began to permeate the air. Deliberately, she turned away from the sketches and paintings and shifted so that she faced him fully, hands clasped tightly in her lap. He hadn't the faintest clue what was about to pass her lips, but he had the feeling it would change everything between them.

She breathed in a deep inhale and released it. "I shall never marry."

This again? "You are the daughter of a family of good reputation. It is quite likely you will marry, and well."

She shook her head, adamant. "I shan't."

But you're so very intelligent and pretty, Will wanted to say, and didn't.

"I've reconciled myself to the fact," she stated.

"It is hardly a fact," he countered.

She squared her shoulders. Here it came. He felt it.

"And there is something I want," she continued, ignoring him.

Twin slivers of dread and excitement stirred inside Will. Violet Hotchkiss had a talent for producing this peculiar blend of feelings. He cleared his throat, matter of fact. "What is it that you want, Miss Hotchkiss?"

"I—I—" She swallowed. "I want to experience what goes on between a man and a woman."

The breath caught in Will's chest. Surely, he hadn't heard her correctly. "You and I are talking," he began, slowly. "*That* goes on between a man and a woman."

Violet exhaled a frustrated sigh. "You are being deliberately obtuse."

"And you are being unreasonable. Surely, you have any number of swain clamoring at your door."

Will held on to his resolve to be reasonable. His body, however, had other ideas about what she might be suggesting.

And there was nothing reasonable about it.

"But what of who *I* want?"

Of a sudden, Will understood. A surge of hot anger flashed through him. "Is this about my dunderheaded cousin Oliver Quincy?"

Violet blinked. He might have asked with a bit too much force. But truly...

"Yes and no," she said.

"Explain," Will commanded before throwing himself into a chair on the opposite side of the room. Distance was needed.

"That night"—she didn't need to explain which night. They both knew—"It truly settled inside me that I shall never have the sort of man *I* want. It's a fact I've accepted, but, still, I want to *know*..." she trailed.

Will kept his silence. The knowledge she wanted was clear. The knowledge of Eve.

And, oh, what a temptation to impart that knowledge.

One he must resist.

"And I thought, well, I thought," she said, "I thought since you did the gentlemanly thing that night, you might do it again."

Will pushed forward in his chair, elbows resting on his knees. Words kept spilling from her mouth in configurations that couldn't possibly be. "The *gentlemanly thing*? You believe I kissed you because I am a gentleman?"

"Yes, of course. Why else would you have kissed me?"

"I can think of another reason."

"Oh?"

"Because I wanted to."

As the admission hung in the air between them, Violet's eyes went wide by slow increments. He'd thrown her off balance. *Good.*

Her eyes narrowed into slits with sudden suspicion. "You do not have to speak falsities."

On a rough exhale, Will flung his weight back into the chair. Was there no getting through to this woman?

For her part, Violet released a sigh—a delicate breath that called to mind another sort of sigh he'd very much like to extract from her—and removed her spectacles. Will only resisted telling her to leave them on. She was lovely without them, but she was adorable with them. He rather liked adorable. But...

How did she not know she was desirable and lovely? Not the flashy lovely of some ladies, like her sister Mrs. Granville. Rather, Violet's loveliness was understated with her radiant skin and eyes bright with curiosity. She was so much more than lovely. She was *attractive.*

She rose to her feet, and a pulse of anticipation traced through Will. Mayhap she'd come to her senses and was readying herself to bid him adieu. That would be the reasonable course of action. He'd almost resigned the unreasonable side of himself to it—the side that didn't want her to come to her senses—when she kicked off one slipper, then the other, and took a step... toward him.

Will shoved forward in his chair, which groaned its displeasure with all the back and forth it was suffering beneath his weight and movement. "What are you thinking?"

She loosened the sash at her waist, and it fluttered to the ground. She took another step. "I'm trying not to think."

"Miss Hotchkiss—"

"*Violet*," she cut him off.

Will nearly emitted a groan of his own. "Violet"—her name emerged as a deep, desperate rasp—"you cannot know what you're about."

Her head canted, familiar curiosity shining bright in her eyes. "Isn't this what men like? I've read books—"

Will held up a hand, effectively stopping the rest of that sentence. He couldn't hear what Violet Hotchkiss had planned for him and hold on to his crumbling resolve. "Yes, men do like that sort of thing." Then his brain caught up to the beginning of her next sentence. "Wait, what books?"

Violet swallowed. "Well, three books to be precise." She cleared her throat. "I do not know their author or titles."

"And the substance of them?" Will had a feeling.

"Well"—Violet's hands clenched and unclenched at her sides—"when Mrs. Acton's husband passed away a few years ago, she asked me to sort through his books for donations to the village library. Deep in the stacks—really hidden away—I happened upon a three volume set, all bound in plain black leather, with no title or author name on the cover or spine."

Will's instinct about the content that lay within those books grew in certainty. "Did you open one?"

Violet nodded.

"And?"

"And I snapped it shut in an instant. It was full of... of—"

"Erotic images?"

Again, she nodded.

"Then what did you do?"

"I, um, opened it again." She gave a small shrug, conveying little apology in the gesture. "It's my curiosity. Once provoked, it won't leave me be." Her tongue swiped across her bottom lip. "It was page after page of women and men engaged in, well, what women and men do in their bedrooms. Actually, very few of the, um, *couplings* took place in bedrooms. And I highly doubt many of them were wed, either."

Will had another question. One it wasn't his business to ask. "What did you do with the books?"

"I couldn't give them to Mrs. Acton or the library, so I, um, took them home."

"*Home?*"

"To my bedroom."

"And your family didn't have a few concerns?"

Violet looked at him as if he'd gone suddenly daft. "I could hardly place them on my bookshelf. I hid them away."

"And never looked at them again?"

Her discomfort was evident. "Not quite."

"Your curiosity?"

She nodded. "There were periods of time—"

Will found his muscles bunching in anticipatory tension.

"—when I indulged my curiosity about them *daily*."

Will could hardly draw breath or utter a word in response. Which was just as well, for Violet was inclined to continue. "Truly, one might call it a brief, rather intense obsession."

Will might not know what to say to her shocking revelations, but his cock knew how to respond. He shifted in his seat to accommodate its increasing girth.

"Those exposed bodies, and what they were doing with one another, well—"

"Impossible to resist," Will supplied for her in a deep rasp.

"Quite."

Her gaze intense upon him, Violet reached around her side, and before Will could comprehend what she was about, she'd unfastened a short row of buttons and her dress was sliding down her body. Then, there she stood before him in her stocking feet wearing only short stays and a chemise that fell to her upper thighs, revealing a tantalizing patch of skin between the bottom hem and the garters holding her stockings.

How he wanted to taste that patch of skin.

He had a decision to make. Tell her to leave or go through with it.

There was no middle.

He knew what was proper, but they had strayed well outside the bounds of propriety, and it wasn't the truest reason he couldn't tell her to leave, anyway.

Standing there with eyes shining bright and fearful, she'd made herself vulnerable to him. Her course of action might be utterly and completely wrongheaded, but it was courageous, too.

He would not leave her alone in this.

This was a risk for her in ways it wasn't for him. It could ruin her.

Well, he wouldn't allow it. There was one established way of preventing such an outcome. Yet...

He didn't want to force her hand in such a manner. If—*when*—that happened, it would be her choice.

But he was getting ahead of himself. In the here and now, well, he wanted her.

Which decided it.

"Remove your stockings," he found himself saying.

She set about the task the way she set about everything—efficiently.

He held up a staying hand. "*Slowly.*"

Chapter Seven

What Violet found in Sinclair's gaze sent a feeling, dark, sinuous and thrilling, racing through her.

It was intense and unknown to her, this feeling, for she'd never been gazed upon so. Her body, however, seemed to have an instinctive understanding of it as a melting occurred within her, a pooling deep in her belly, and deeper still so it was all she could do not to squeeze her thighs together.

This was *desire.*

While she'd seen the acts of copulation on the page, this feeling couldn't be depicted. It could only be experienced.

Slowly, with a tremor in her fingers, she began rolling down her stocking, his gaze fast upon each deliberate inch revealed. She flicked the stocking toward him, and he snatched it out of the air, mid-flutter. All without taking his eyes off her.

Oh.

She hadn't known it would be like this. That it would *feel* like this inside her body, tingly and fluttery and exhilarating.

And the man hadn't even touched her yet.

Her fingers hooked on to her other stocking, and she stopped. A boldness surged inside her. It wanted to upset his balance, to test him and see what he was made of. "Perhaps you can do better?"

The breath froze in her chest. How had she asked such a... *brazen*... question?

His fingers steepled contemplatively before him, his head cocked, and an assessing light entered his eye. He, too, was evaluating what she was made of. "Is that a challenge?"

A thrill shivered through her. She desired nothing more than to see how he could do better, for she harbored no doubt that he could. She licked her bottom lip, a nervous little flick, and nodded.

On a growl, he sprang off his chair. Before she could comprehend what he was about, he'd scooped her up into his arms and was marching her through the cottage. Unable to help herself, Violet turned her face into his chest, closed her eyes, and inhaled. Sandalwood and warmth and man. *Sinclair.*

They entered a dark room, lit only by the moonlight streaming in through the window. Sinclair's bedroom. He released her legs, and her arms reached instinctively around his neck. As her toes found purchase on dense Persian wool below, her body brushed the full length of him. He had no give as she swayed forward. *Rigid. Muscular.* An object pressed into her belly. It was—*oh*—his manhood. *Thick. Hard.*

His fingers tucked beneath her chin, and his face angled down. It was only when he hesitated, his lips but a slender inch from hers, his breath warm against her skin, that she realized she'd been starving for this these last two months, for his kiss. On a famished moan, she pushed up against him, his hardness turning her legs to jelly, and claimed his lips for herself. *Soft. Firm. Delicious.* His tongue slipped past her lips, playfully inviting her to tangle with him.

Violet's inhibitions began to fall away. She was exactly where she should be, in this man's arms. Though she understood her actions to be wrong, so, too, could she not help feeling their very rightness.

His large hands clutched her waist and lifted her off the ground before depositing her on the edge of the high bed, her legs dangling off the side. When he fell to his knees and gazed up at her, lust in his eyes, she never felt so sensual, so *powerful*, as if she held the fate of this man in the palm of her hand.

Bold... Womanly... Transformed. Utterly and completely unlike herself. That was how she felt in this moment.

He touched her inner thigh and trailed a long finger along its sensitive skin, before snagging on her garter, then tugging the stocking down and off. He caught her foot in his hand, and his gaze burned a trail up the length of her leg, hitching on the hem of her chemise, which only reached far enough to preserve her modesty.

Or did it? The wicked smile curving along his lips told a different story.

She squirmed beneath his scrutiny, unsure if discomfort was the cause or... *impatience.*

His gaze flew up to meet hers. "You're certain?"

Oh, the velvety rasp of his words against his throat. It raised goose bumps along her skin, tightening her nipples into hard buds. Anticipatory nerves fluttered through her, and she gave a solemn nod. "In all my life, I've never been more so."

He shifted forward, his shoulder nudging her other leg as he continued to move closer. Her breath caught in her lungs. What was he—

"Do you trust me?"

She nodded, speech lost to her. It was the accumulation of the man. His mass. His scent. His heat. *Him.*

He bent his head and... *oh!* He licked her inner thigh.

"Sinclair," she gasped, "are *you* certain?" She hadn't thought to ask him the question.

He chuckled, the sound deep and rumbly in his chest. Strangely, Violet felt reassured. She'd put herself in the hands of a man who knew his way around a woman's body. The thought sent a quiver of lust shooting straight through her.

He stroked his tongue along the sensitive flesh. Higher he moved, pushing the hem of her chemise, revealing her soft mound of curls. "Perfection," he murmured, his gaze flashing to meet hers, his eyes dark and inscrutable for that quick moment.

He shifted higher, as if he was about to—*Oh!*

The shock—the pleasure!—that soared through her as his tongue glided along the slit of her most intimate flesh. The breath caught in her chest as she collapsed back on her elbows. He did it again. An animal groan tore from her. She hardly recognized herself. Who was this wanton, spreading her legs wider, all but pleading with Sinclair to keep performing the magic he was working upon her body?

For that was what coursed through her veins,

sending sparks of pleasure along every nerve ending. *Magic.*

Unconsciously, she reached out and wove her fingers through his thick hair, the feeling in her sex building with intensity, making her gasp and groan as his tongue, firm and soft and—*oh*—so talented, laved, stroked, flicked, caressed, and brought her body to a state she never knew it capable of as a force began to build behind the pleasure.

His hands clamped around her hips, stabilizing her. Had she been writhing beneath him? She cared not. All she had room for in her consciousness was this pleasure, and her yearning, straining, striving for *more*.

A greedy feeling began to claw at her, and she clenched his hair into a fist as the feeling intensified, her entire being condensed into the place where the tip of his tongue touched her. Her sex, wound so tight with anticipation, released in an explosion of sensation. Pleasure, intense and wild, overtook her in rippling waves, causing her to cry out with abandon. By increments, the intensity faded, leaving in its wake a buzzing in her body, which had been reduced to naught more than an enervated bundle of satiety.

Yet, came an unbidden thought, *there is more.* She knew it. She'd seen it depicted on the pages of those naughty books.

And she wanted it.

Somehow, she found the strength to push upright, planting one hand, then the other behind her. A few feet away, Sinclair had sunk back on his haunches. "I can stop there," he said, his tone as guarded as his eyes.

"Don't you dare consider such a thing, Will Sinclair."

She reached out and grabbed his cravat, unknotting it in a matter of seconds. His shirt flopped open, revealing his chest, muscled and dusted with a light coating of hair. "So... mmm," she said, discernable words lost to her. Sinclair was just *so... mmm.*

The next thing she knew, she was lifting the shirt over his head and his arms were around her, untying her stays and tossing the garment aside, then lifting the chemise over her head and hastily discarding that, too. Seconds later, she was fully naked and he was standing before her, down to his trousers.

Her mouth went dry at the sight of him—broad shoulders, muscled chest, ridged stomach, trail of hair that narrowed as it led the eye down, down, down to the waistband of his trousers and lower still to the closure. Body aquiver, she touched trembly fingers to his stomach. Oh, the feel of his skin and the muscles beneath as they tensed in response. Gratifying, that reaction.

Her fingers followed the same trail her eyes had, to

the waistband and lower. She became distracted by what she found throbbing beneath superfine wool: his manhood, rigid and long. She traced its hard length, her heart racing. It was so... *big*. "How can *this* possibly—?" She bit off the rest of the question.

But he intuited it, for his wicked smile returned. "Would you like to find out?"

Anticipation flared hot inside her, and all she could do was nod as she watched him unfasten the closure. Seconds later, he was as naked as she. *Adonis.*

She'd never dreamed a man could be so beautiful. She was a virgin, it was true, but her body knew exactly how to respond to him. It was lit on fire.

And the way his eyes roved over her naked form... *Ravenous.*

That a man—*this* man—could look at her so. A confidence in her femininity surged within her, something she had never experienced.

He moved forward, slowly, deliberately, one hand finding the nape of her neck, the other the small of her back, and continued moving until she lay beneath him on her back, his body hovering above. The space between and around them grew in intimacy. They were the only two people in the world who could exist in this place, for it was they who had created it.

Instinctively, Violet's legs spread, inviting him to

settle between. She felt *it*—his manhood—hot and weighty against her quim. It wasn't until she felt the press of his weight that she realized how hungry her body had been for the heavy feel of him, his skin sticky against hers, their breaths mingled, their eyes locked. The world could stop spinning round the sun, and they would never know it.

Uncertainty flashed within his eyes. He needed her to say it again.

"I want this." *I want you, only you*, she barely stopped herself from saying.

"It will hurt," he said, the words rumbling through her.

She nodded.

Gently, he cupped one breast. "So sweet," he said, before bending his head and taking the nipple in his mouth. Her head arced back with blind pleasure as his tongue slid and flicked across the sensitive skin. Lower, he touched her until his finger was a wet slide along her slit, sending yet more flames of desire licking through her. Her hips gave an impatient swivel.

On a low laugh, he said, "You are so wet."

His manhood pressed at the opening of her sex, insistent, hot, until he gave a swift thrust and pierced her maidenhead, eliciting a sharp, "Oh!" from Violet. As one, their bodies went still, even as his eyes searched hers, then the pain settled and faded as quickly as it had come. On its heels arrived that greedy hunger, again clawing at her. Her nails dug into his shoulders, and her back arched, anything to bring her closer to what she wanted, *needed*, which was more of him.

It was as if she'd been created for this.

He chuckled. "So impatient."

As he began moving inside her, stroke by measured stroke, one hand cupped her face, bringing her mouth to his, and the other beneath her hips, steadying her as he slid in and out, a slow, relentless rhythm that called to a madness inside her. Driven by instinct, her hips joined his in the rhythm, and he groaned, the sound velvet sandpaper, increasing her lust. Her hands explored his splendid body, his thick hair, his muscular shoulders, back, buttocks... Oh, his buttocks.

"Violet"—oh, the sound of her name on his lips— "you are so"—he thrust, she gasped—"*so*"—he thrust again, she moaned—"so *perfect*."

Violet knew she would want to think about that later, but not now, not while the stars in her veins were expanding their light inside her, all her senses concentrated in the places he touched her—his breath at the crook of her neck, one hand clutched at her hip, the other in her hair, and his manhood, oh, his manhood, the pleasure it was delivering... "Oh, Sinclair."

"*Will*," he ground out.

"*Will*," she repeated, his given name yet another intimacy forged.

Her fingernails dug deeper into his back, and he responded by increasing his rhythm. Her body had never felt like such a wonder, so capable of experiencing and giving pleasure.

"Violet, I can't go on much longer."

"Then—*oh*—then don't," she gasped.

Their bodies slicked with mingled sweat, it was as if all their inhibitions had been given permission to run free. An unrelenting quality entered the way he took her, his gaze holding hers captive as the build to release began its climb. He reached down and stroked the nub of her sex, the place his tongue had so expertly caressed minutes ago. And that was all she needed to tumble over the edge into oblivion, her sex clenching and releasing, shooting pleasure through her in tight pulses.

Relentless, he drove inside her, his eyes glazed with desire, all his muscles straining with tension, lost in the abandon of pleasure. Suddenly, he arched back and pulled off her. Unable to stifle the protest, she cried out. His glistening, glorious body bathed in moonlight, his head tipped back, he spilled his seed away from her as a long animal moan tore from his parted mouth. Enervated, he collapsed beside her, and she curled into his side, the position a natural fit. He pulled her tighter to him, and his arm remained, its weight heavy and secure and *right*.

As she drifted into the waters of thoroughly sated slumber, a thought met her. This joining was not merely about the body. It involved the soul, too.

She hadn't expected that.

He should wake her.

Will knew he must.

But he couldn't yet bring himself to do it, not with her head nestled into the crook of his shoulder like the perfect puzzle piece, as if they were made for one another.

He stopped the thought before it could gain momentum and explore places that weren't possible. She didn't view him in that way.

Right.

"Violet," he whispered.

Dark eyelashes resting contently on her cheeks, her lips curled into a sated, delicious smile. It was all he could do not to press his mouth to hers.

"Violet," he repeated.

This time, her eyes fluttered open, soft and

unguarded. She'd never looked at him so. Warmth began to spread through him. Then her brow furrowed, and he sensed a shift in the moment. Now she was thinking. Thinking too much, more like.

Her eyes went wide, and she sat straight upright. "What is the time?" Her legs were already swinging off the bed.

Will reached for the pocket watch on his bedside table. "Half past eight."

Violet emitted a small cry, hopped to the floor, and began scurrying around, chemise over her head, one stocking already halfway up her leg. At a much slower, and more reasonable, pace, Will snatched up his trousers and jerked them on. He had no right to the annoyance he felt—after all, it was her reputation that would suffer the most should they be discovered—yet it wouldn't subside. Now that she'd used him for what she'd come for, she couldn't get away from him fast enough.

She pulled her stays over her head and frantically reached behind her back in a futile attempt to tie them. Will cocked a hip on the bed and watched, and waited. She twisted around, her impatient gaze meeting his over her shoulder. "Can you assist me?"

Wordlessly, Will sauntered over, performed the task, and stepped back.

When she swiveled to face him, Will couldn't hold back a smile. "Your hair might require some attention."

On a huff of frustration, she raced to the room's lone mirror and tucked all the loose tendrils into place. Again, she faced him, looking very much her customary self. Too much so. Already, Will yearned for the Violet of an hour past.

A question occurred to him. "Where do your family think you?"

A sheepishness entered her expression. "At my sister's house."

"And where does your sister think you?"

Her gaze shifted. "She thinks me at home."

Will couldn't believe she'd failed to devise any sort of plan. "How long do you think that lie will stand?"

Violet flicked her wrist dismissively. "I shall go directly to Lily's from here and tell her I lost track of the time on a ramble."

"It's full dark."

"It's the sort of thing I did all the time as a girl."

"I remember."

Her eyebrows lifted. "You do?"

He nodded, and the moment grew soft. "It wasn't unusual for me to espy you from afar on occasion." He wouldn't mention that he'd followed her, too, on more than one occasion. Usually, when he saw her out near dusk and needed to see her home, safe.

"Sinclair—"

"Will."

"*Will.*" She bit her bottom lip nervously. "About tonight, I must thank—"

"Do *not* thank me," he demanded, an unaccountable anger bubbling up.

Again, her brow furrowed.

"What happened here tonight was not a gift or a favor or whatever you think in that topsy-turvy head of yours. What happened in that bed"—he pointed for emphasis—"was mutual. I wanted you, and you wanted me. Understood?"

Slowly, mouth slightly agape, she nodded.

"Now, let's get you to Granville Court."

"There is no need for you to escort me all that way."

"Would you like to go by carriage or foot?" he asked, ignoring the blasted, frustrating woman.

"Truly—"

"By carriage or foot?"

"By foot," she relented, at last.

"Then let us start walking."

They were out the door in mere minutes, only stopping long enough for Violet to find her spectacles and hastily don her dress, other stocking, slippers, and light wool cape. Not a word was spoken between them on the twenty minute walk.

Once arrived within sight of Granville Court, Violet stopped. "'Tis best if we part ways here."

Will offered her a shallow bow, even as his feet remained firmly planted.

Violet's fists found her hips. "You are going to watch me all the way to the house, aren't you?"

"Yes."

It wasn't until Granville Court's front door closed behind Violet that Will pivoted on his heel and strode down the path from whence they'd come, the quiet of the night closing in around him. On the walk back to his cottage, however, his mind was anything but silent.

She'd been about to *thank* him for servicing her. As much as that in itself annoyed and frustrated Will, there was something else that he sensed and liked even less. Violet held a surprising lack of belief in herself. Not in her mental capabilities—that certainty she had in abundance—but in herself as a woman possessed of sensuality and allure.

It was that which had motivated her almost spoken thank you, and it turned his stomach.

What was more, and slightly infuriating, she hadn't demanded anything of him after her ravishment. Didn't she understand it was her right to do so?

Provoking woman.

He wanted her to make demands of him. For there was much he wanted to give her, freely, and not just his body.

But that, too.

Now, to make her see reason. Unlike in the months following their kiss on the night of the Twelfth Night Ball, he wouldn't leave her be. He would persist.

Tonight only marked the beginning of his pursuit of Violet Hotchkiss.

Only she didn't know it yet.

Chapter Eight

Palms sweaty and his heart a heavy thud in his chest, Will strode up the lane toward Hotchkiss House.

He hadn't been invited, that was the thing. But what he was pulling behind him, Violet needed. He only hoped she would see it the same way. The frustrating woman had a habit of taking the view—any view—opposite of his.

Will had entered the circle drive in front of the house when a rider emerged from around the side. Mr. Hotchkiss called out, "Whoa," reining in his mount. "Sinclair, did I forget an engagement this morning?"

Will shook his head, at once feeling like a sheepish young man. "You haven't, sir. I'm here to deliver a—" He bit off the rest of the sentence. *Gift to Violet.* He couldn't very well say that. Mr. Hotchkiss might get the wrong idea.

Or would it be the *right* idea?

"A hand drawn wagon, is it?" Mr. Hotchkiss's eyes narrowed on the conveyance. "With four wheels and a single pull?"

"It is. Yes." Will tried not to shuffle his feet. "I believe this would be of some considerable use to Miss Hotchkiss during her book deliveries."

Mr. Hotchkiss's gaze went narrow and assessing, and Will felt his measure being taken. "How attentive of you, Sinclair."

Will caught a speculative note in that *attentive.*

Mr. Hotchkiss called out over his shoulder, "Smith, inform Mrs. Hotchkiss that Mr. Sinclair is paying a call" —he shot Will another appraising glance—"on Miss Hotchkiss."

"I can leave it—" Will's suggestion was cut short when the front door swung open and out stepped Miss Hotchkiss—*Violet*—her arms heavily laden with a thick stack of books.

"Papa," she called out, "I thought you would have already taken to the road if you're to be back—" Her gaze landed on Will, and she stopped dead in her tracks, both walking and talking.

Will hadn't prepared himself for the sight of her. She looked her customary fresh and bright self, properly dressed in an ivory muslin morning gown and pink wool pelisse, spectacles perched upon her straight nose. But now that he knew her beyond this surface, his mind couldn't help filling in what wasn't on display for the world to see.

He knew the gentle line of her hip. He knew the sweet curve of her breasts. He knew the scent of her, rose and woman. He knew her cry of pleasure.

He *knew* this woman, all the intimate parts of her.

Mr. Hotchkiss tipped his hat. "Right you are, my dear. I shall be off." With that, the old gentleman set out, leaving Will and Violet alone.

"Mr. Sinclair," she said with a shy note in her voice.

"Miss Hotchkiss," he replied, returning the formality.

Her gaze fell upon the wagon. "Have you a delivery? Perhaps for the stables?"

Will shook his head. "For you."

Violet's brow lifted.

"The wagon would be of some considerable use to you on your Tuesday library rounds," Will explained. Never had he felt like such a sputtering green youth, not even when he'd been one.

"I've told you that I have no need of such assistance."

The books shifted precariously in her arms, belying her words.

"Could you, at least, give it a try?"

A moment passed, then another. He could see that she was exasperated, but he'd made a reasonable case for the wagon. There was no denying it.

At last, she nodded her acceptance and crossed the distance between them. As she drew near, Will's heart doubled the rate of its beats. It couldn't seem to help itself. The hope that she liked it wouldn't leave him be.

Again, he felt like a green youth. It had ever been so with Violet Hotchkiss.

Standing back from the wagon, she cast an assessing eye over it. "'Tis a most unusual conveyance. Its wheels are larger than I've seen, and its bed more shallow. Where did you procure it?"

"I didn't."

"Then how did you come by it?"

"I modified it."

Violet blinked. "*You?*"

Will gave a dismissive shrug. "It didn't take much effort. Just a little imagination."

Her head tipped to the side. "I've never seen its like."

Gratification streaked through Will at the delight that sounded in her declaration. "I believe it light enough for you to pull with ease, hence the large wheels, too."

Her violet eyes shone with pleasure behind her spectacles. "How very considerate of you."

"It was nothing."

Violet began carefully arranging the books in the wagon bed. Once she'd finished, Will held out the pull. "Would you like to try it?"

When she reached for the handle, their fingers brushed. Even through kidskin gloves, Will's skin sparked alive at the point of contact. A mirroring reaction shone in her eyes. *Intimacy. Knowledge.*

The moment stretched a beat too long before she delicately cleared her throat, and her gaze skittered away. "I thank you for your consideration, but I am sure you have a day to get on with."

She was all but dismissing him outright, which only brought out the contrarian in Will. "I don't have anywhere else to be."

Or would rather be, he didn't say.

They had taken no more than twenty steps when Will asked, "How does the wagon maneuver? Is it heavy for you to pull?"

"I hardly feel it. Again, thank you."

"Your gratitude is hardly necessary," he said, a gruffness in the reply. Would the woman never stop thanking him?

He didn't want simple gratitude.

He wanted something altogether more complex.

He glanced around to give the wagon a quick inspection when he noticed the book at the top of the stack. Part of him knew he should let it lie, but a larger part couldn't resist the pursuit. He needed to know what she thought. "That book looks rather new," he said, pointing.

Violet took quick note of the book before casting him an amused glance. "Do you keep abreast on the latest offerings in children's literature?"

A fair bit of teasing. Will didn't mind.

She said, "I take it you are referring to Sir Pug?"

"I am."

"I hadn't heard of him either until a month ago when *Sir Pug Goes To Town* appeared on our doorstep. Then a few days ago, *Sir Pug Explores the Stables* arrived. The children will be delighted."

"They enjoy it?"

Her face lit up. "They adore Sir Pug. Actually," she said, her head canting, "there is something about the books I think you would appreciate."

"What is that?"

"The watercolor drawings are done with exquisite care."

Gratification spread through Will. Now would be the time to tell her. But she kept speaking, "With your talent, you could aspire to something like them."

It was all Will could do not to snort. "Vi—" He bit off the rest of her name. As absurd as it sounded, he wanted to court her properly. "Miss Hotchkiss, I must confess something to you."

Her brow lifted in silent query. However, before Will could speak another word, a voice cried out, "Miss Hotchkiss! Miss Hotchkiss!"

Will and Violet turned in unison to find a maid racing up the lane toward them. "Colleen, what is it?" Violet returned with no small amount of alarm.

The servant skidded to a stop and paused a moment to catch her heaving breath, wisps of hair clinging to the perspiration on her cheeks. "Mrs. Hotchkiss sent me to walk with you."

Will detected the tension release from Violet's shoulders. "Ah."

Will understood, too. He and Violet walking together, alone, was a breach of Society's rules for befitting conduct. He noticed they had reached the outskirts of Bumpstead Hollow, and he'd accomplished what he set out to do, which was deliver the wagon to Violet. "I should take my—"

"Leave?" she finished for him.

"Aye."

"Don't." Sincerity shone out from her eyes. "Stay."

Stay.

Will's insides went light and variable, the pleasure of that simple word, of the plea within it, stealing through his veins.

He hadn't considered she might desire his company.

She'd asked him to stay.

Violet could hardly countenance how she'd mustered the courage.

She had been bold three nights ago in his cottage, but, somehow, this felt bolder, like she had more at stake. As if what happened between two bodies wasn't nearly as vital as what happened between two minds. It was no wonder that most poetry was composed about the relations between men and women. It was a dratted confusing business.

Sinclair—*Will*, he'd insisted—nodded, and a strain Violet hadn't realized she was holding, released. As they resumed their progress, with Colleen some ten feet at their back, Violet kept her eyes trained steadfastly straight ahead. Yet she couldn't seem to keep the periphery of her vision off him. Now that they'd done... *that*... together, she knew him in a way she hadn't anticipated when she'd made the decision to enter his cottage.

In truth, it had given her a different way of viewing the world, and men and women in particular. All couples had this secret knowledge of one another, not just of the body, but of the soul. Lily and Mr. Granville. Even her parents, though she had no interest in pursuing that thought further. The story of Adam and Eve made altogether much more sense now that she could view it from this altered perspective.

Three nights ago, she had taken a bite of the apple, thinking it would be enough to sustain her for a lifetime. Now, she wasn't sure one bite was enough to satisfy her for a week of days, or nights. Particularly when Will arrived on her doorstep with a gift in hand, looking so utterly delicious. She could only wonder how amenable he would be to another bite.

As they entered Bumpstead Hollow and the flow of its high street's dozy morning hustle and bustle, he smiled down at her. "Where is our first stop?"

Violet had opened her mouth to answer him when a familiar figure appeared in the distance. Could it be?

She squinted. It could, and it was.

Mr. Quincy.

Her stomach sinking to her toes, she shot Will a quick glance. He hadn't yet noticed, but he must have seen a change in her eyes for his gaze cut forward. The muscles of his jaw worked into a tight clench, and his eyes narrowed.

"Cousin!" Mr. Quincy called out, waving, his pinched mouth only just releasing into a thin smile.

Violet had never taken note of his superior air before now, but, thinking back, she realized it had ever been so. Nervously, she glanced again at Will, but his face had gone to stone and utterly unreadable.

A few moments later, Mr. Quincy had reached them and was giving Violet a shallow, perfunctory bow. "Miss Hotchkiss."

"Mr. Quincy," she returned, but his attention had already shifted to Will. She couldn't help feeling she'd been dismissed as superfluous to the proceedings. A cat whose fur had been brushed the wrong direction likely felt this way.

"Sinclair, I have news," Mr. Quincy announced.

"Oh?" How aloof and dismissive Will not only sounded, but appeared, too. Had he always regarded his cousin in this manner? Violet rather thought so.

Mr. Quincy continued on, "I have secured the Houghton estate. Our mammas will be most pleased to be within a few miles of one another, I dare say."

"Quite," Will bit out, refusing to let Violet catch his eye.

Mr. Quincy flicked a piece of lint off his impeccable sleeve. If a man could wear his clothes too well, it was Mr. Quincy. There was simply too much refinement and elegance to him. Too much of the dandy.

Will, on the other hand, his clothes were well-made, and within fashion, but they didn't appear as if he gave them more than a few minutes' consideration before donning them. For that, he wore his toggery all the better.

"What brings you into the village, old chap?" Mr. Quincy asked.

Will indicated the wagon behind them.

Mr. Quincy's mouth curved into a small frown. "Did you purchase it?" he asked.

"It is Tuesday," Will all but growled in his deep baritone voice.

"'Tis," Mr. Quincy replied in a clipped, high-pitched syllable. The supercilious expression on his face implied he'd reached the conclusion that his cousin had gone a bit addlepated.

Will and Mr. Quincy were each other's opposite in every way. And Will was the superior man for it. There was simply no denying it.

How had Violet not seen this from the start? Wasn't it obvious to anyone with eyes and ears?

"'Tis the day Miss Hotchkiss makes her library rounds," Will explained.

Mr. Quincy gave a start of surprise. "Library rounds? Whatever for?"

Violet felt a blush rise. Mr. Quincy didn't remember. Of course not. He'd never truly listened in the first place. "It is something I do with the village children," she found herself explaining. "I have noticed that the earlier they start reading—"

Mr. Quincy chortled dismissively. "That cannot be a good use of your energies, Miss Hotchkiss. Take it from me: we have our place, and they have theirs. Best leave them to it."

Violet faced Will. "Mr. Sinclair," she asked, a question pushing forward that wouldn't be contained, "what think you of my library?"

Although annoyance still shone in Will's deep blue gaze, so, too, did a warming occur when he fixed his gaze upon her. "As experiments go—"

"*Experiments?*" Violet cut in, affronted. "You think my library a social experiment? Like something Mr. Robert Malthus would have theorized?" Violet's outrage built with each question she asked, betrayal running through her. "This is not play, and I do not toy with people's lives."

Will shook his head. "Not in the mode of Malthus, no."

"Who in the heavens, pray tell, is Mr. Robert Malthus?" interjected Mr. Quincy.

His question only confirmed it for Violet. Mr. Quincy truly was a dolt. There was no excuse for an educated gentleman not to know Mr. Malthus's writings on population growth and economics.

Will ignored his cousin. "Mayhap I spoke wrongly when I used the word experiment. I believe *endeavor* is more correct. And, Miss Hotchkiss"—his gaze was direct and sincere and magnetic—"'tis a worthwhile one."

"Oh, cousin, you mustn't encourage her," Mr. Quincy said, even as he barely suppressed a yawn. "Reading is the sort of thing that only incites dissatisfaction amongst the masses, and who needs that bother on their lands?"

Violet didn't give Mr. Quincy's bleatings an ounce of attention as she addressed Will. "I've always thought so," she said, a bit breathless. Had his eyes always been such an intriguing blue? She must stop swimming in their deep pools, or she would make a spectacle of herself.

"Efforts like yours will not only benefit Bumpstead

Hollow," he declared, "but all of England for generations to come."

Violet hadn't only become lost in Will's eyes, but in his words, too. That he thought so of her and her efforts filled her with warmth and delight, and longing, too.

One night with him wasn't enough.

She wanted more of this man who surprised her anew with each encounter. All these years, she never knew Will Sinclair, not truly, not the genuine him who existed below his perfect, too-tall, too-massive, too-handsome surface. She'd judged him by his looks and his social status, but not by his true measure.

If this moment were a scene from one of her beloved novels, she would be realizing that it was Will who was the hero of the story. Which made Mr. Quincy the... *rake?* She stifled a snort. Not bloody likely. An altogether character for Mr. Quincy came to mind, the buffoon.

"Cousin," the buffoon sputtered, "have you developed a radical bent? I always thought those travels of yours would put funny ideas into your head."

Will snorted at his cousin's alarm. "You might try not thinking too much, Quincy."

Mr. Quincy adjusted the knot of his cravat. "Mamma always says so."

Will flashed Violet an amused glance, which she returned. What had she ever seen in Mr. Quincy?

A mollified Mr. Quincy continued, "Speaking of the good of England, cousin, about the Houghton estate." The man had an unparalleled ability of remaining oblivious to all but his own concerns.

Will's face went dark. "What about it?"

"It seems that I shall be in need of a steward. Does your man oversee multiple estates in the area?"

"He does," Will replied, a guardedness in his tone.

"Ah, well then, there we have it. Is he on your estate today?"

"He is," Will said, a touch regretfully.

Mr. Quincy's face lit up. "I must start up to Town later today, so now would be the best time."

"The best time?" Will's brow furrowed. "For what?"

"For you to introduce me to your steward, of course."

The presumption of Mr. Quincy. Really, it was so astonishing, it was almost admirable. But it was none of Violet's affair to manage. Deciding to leave the cousins to it and get on with her day, she silently signaled Colleen.

"I never agreed—" Will had begun and stopped. "What are you doing, Miss Hotchkiss?"

"I have books to deliver, and I am already late."

Will opened his mouth to protest, but Violet cut him

off. "And your dear cousin needs you." She couldn't keep the tease out of her voice.

"'Tis true, old chap," Mr. Quincy agreed.

"But, Miss Hotchkiss, don't *you* need me?" Will asked, his voice gone low and gravelly.

A shiver ran through Violet. His question was asking so much more, and, oh, how she longed to say *yes.* "I believe you have already helped me with all my needs," she said instead.

"Now that's all settled," Mr. Quincy inserted. "Cousin?"

Will's gaze remained stubbornly fixed on Violet. "*All* of them?"

Heat flushed through her, and a feeling pooled deep in her belly, and lower still. She'd been introduced to this feeling, intimately. *Desire.* "Should any further needs arise," she began, her mouth suddenly dry, "I shall come to you directly."

His gaze held hers captive for the time it took her heart to pound three rapid beats. "See that you do."

Will offered her a shallow bow of farewell, and Mr. Quincy followed hasty suit. Violet gave a nod, not so much silent as speechless.

As she continued her progress up the high street, pulling the wagon behind her, Colleen at her side, Violet could only trust that her exterior remained cool and implacable and didn't betray the riot of emotion currently storming through her.

Had she truly had the conversation she thought she'd had with Will Sinclair?

Her body, hot and liquid, and her heart, fluttery and racing, knew the answer.

Would she—*could* she seek him out again?

And not simply for his body, but for... *him?*

So, too, did her body—and her heart—know the answer to that question.

Chapter Nine

S *loosh-whoosh... sloosh-whoosh...* On Will punted down the placid river, the only disturbance the small waves rippling out from his oars and the skiff. Light mist disintegrated in the golden morning sun, offering relief from the chilly snap in the air.

It was, in short, the perfect morning for a row.

Sweat pinpricked his skin, and he experienced deep satisfaction at the feel of exertion in his body, this testing of himself. English gentlemen often possessed the physique of a veal calf, tender and soft. Upon his return to England, Will had determined he wouldn't be that sort of gentleman. He needed to feel his body working and proving what it could do. How else was a man to feel strong and capable, rather than weak and coddled?

One such weak and coddled gentleman entered his mind. Oliver Quincy. Conceited, ineffectual man.

Will put a little extra vigor into his pull and the skiff shot backward, frightening a raft of ducks into a fractious flapping of their wings. The blasted man had to ruin what had been shaping into a perfect morning with Violet. Quincy simply couldn't help himself. It had ever been so.

Yet Will didn't feel all was lost. She had been appreciative of his gift of the wagon. He'd seen it in her smile.

But it was the last few moments of their conversation that had caught hold in his mind and wouldn't let go. The look in her eyes when they'd spoken of her needs. He'd detected more than a passing interest, but rather a hunger that only inflamed his own.

He wanted to explore Violet Hotchkiss's *needs*, every last one of them, until he'd both sated and incited them to more wanting.

His cock swelled, and he rowed yet harder, the skiff obeying his command as it raced across the water. It was one thing that he couldn't get his mind to stray far from Violet, but it was a whole other matter now that his body knew her intimately.

The boathouse, which had been a simple gamekeeper's hut long ago, slid into view at his right. When he'd started rowing during his years at Oxford, a covered dock had been added on the hut. On a brisk morning, like this one, Will was grateful for the servant who banked a fire in the one-room structure every night. After a morning row, he would tie off the boat and settle in with a pot of tea for an hour or so of sketching and painting.

In fact, this morning, he had a few new ideas for Sir Pug that he'd been toying around with. Quick on the heels of that thought came a familiar flare of frustration. He should have told Violet that he was E.B. McWoof when he'd had the chance.

Truly, he'd no notion of creating Sir Pug to begin with. After the ball, he'd resolved to put Violet Hotchkiss behind him. But her circulating library for children started prodding at him, and he wondered how she came by books. Then, one day he'd been sketching, and Sir Pug appeared. Soon, the jaunty dog's adventures were unfolding beneath Will's hand. Within weeks, a completed book was being delivered to Hotchkiss House. Anonymously.

The next time he saw Violet, he would tell her the truth of it. First thing, no distractions.

The opening of the covered dock yawned before him, like a small dark cave. He pulled the oars out of the water and allowed the skiff to glide inside on its own momentum. As his eyes began adjusting to the dim light, he detected a shadowed figure and assumed it was a servant. However, he quickly saw the person wasn't a servant at all.

There stood Violet, leaning against the back wall, her serious gaze fixed on him. And the expression she held for him in her eyes, well, there was no mistaking it. *Desire.*

The Violet Hotchkiss he'd known all his life had never once gazed upon him so. But this Violet was an altogether different proposition.

He longed to bask in the heat of her desire, except for a thought that wouldn't stop nagging at him and let him be. In his heart of hearts, he wanted her to crave more than his body and the pleasure he could bring her.

He wanted her to yearn for all of him.

The skiff eased into the dock, and Will hopped out and tied it off. Straightening, he saw that her gaze hadn't wavered, if anything, it had only intensified. He took one step, then another, moving slowly, as if not to scare her away. "Is there something you need, Violet?"

Her eyes shone bright behind her spectacles. "How very disingenuous of you," she said, breathless, her words carrying no farther than the few feet that now separated them.

Will planted a hand on the patch of wall beside her head. The universe collapsed down to the two of them. "Has a *need* arisen, then?" he asked, liking this game.

She released a trembly breath and whispered into the intimate space between their mouths, "And only you can satisfy it."

Was that a plea he detected in her voice?

Slowly, deliberately, he angled his head and lowered it. Her mouth straining up to meet his—Will couldn't deny the gratification that streaked through him at a Violet unable to contain herself—their lips met. She opened her mouth to be ravished and released a soft moan. Will pressed forward, giving her what she was asking for.

Her hands found his neck, her fingernails scraping along the fine hairs and making them stand on end. Her back arched, pressing the full length of her— breasts, hips—into him. Now it was Will's turn to moan.

How sweet was the taste of her.

How right was the feel of her.

Propriety reared its annoying head. They needed to get inside the boathouse lest they were seen.

Without taking his mouth from hers, Will felt along the wall until he had the door handle in hand. One twist and the door swung inward. He grabbed her hips and began to guide her. Intuiting his intention, she followed his lead, never breaking from his lips, her hands now pulling the shirt from his trousers and roaming freely across his chest and back. It was as if they couldn't feel enough of him.

He kicked the door shut behind them. Already, he'd unbuttoned her pelisse and was now pushing the garment off her shoulders. It was left unnoticed on the floor as he guided her toward the hearth where the banked fire burned low. Her hands were tugging at his shirt.

They had to break the kiss to pull it over his head. Her pupils flared with desire, pushing the irises into thin violet rings. "You are impossibly gorgeous."

Carefully, Will took her spectacles by the bridge and removed them, placing them on the nearest flat surface. He didn't want them breaking during what he had planned.

Never had he felt such urgency for a woman. He saw the same response in her lust-glazed eyes. All that mattered was this moment and each other.

"Turn around," he rasped.

He made short work of the buttons of her dress and slid it off her shoulders, allowing the garment to fall in a pool at her feet, leaving her vulnerable to the sweep of his gaze. He took in her creamy shoulders, back that narrowed to her supple waist, her pert bottom that filled out her chemise to perfection. Slight tremor in his hands, he reached for the knot of her stays. Lacing loosened, he shimmied the garment down her body.

She met his gaze over her shoulder, a nervy, expectant look in her eye, before turning to face him fully. Rosy nipples puckered beneath the gossamer muslin of her chemise. Without a hesitating thought, he angled forward and cupped her sweet breasts, catching one hard bud between his lips through fabric. A long, primal groan escaped Violet, and her back arched to offer him more.

He sucked, eliciting a swift intake of breath. When his tongue flicked, her breath released in a sharp burst. Her abandoned response to him only increased the anticipation surging through his veins, making him tremble with a lust that might never know satiety.

Her hands felt for his shoulders and gave a push. Now it was she who was guiding him. When the backs of his legs hit the chair nearest the hearth, he dropped into the seat, and she stared down at him. Only he knew her, this wanton Violet.

He reached for the closure of his trousers, and her bottom lip caught between her teeth. She watched as he slipped out one button after another until, at last, the fall opened and there was his manhood, hard and ready. A dark, sinuous energy permeated the air as the rise and fall of her chest went shallow, a mirror of his.

She angled over him, and her hands found purchase on his shoulders as her knees wedged into the chair to either side of him, her sleek legs now straddling his thighs. Above him, she hovered, her scent of roses and woman encircling him, drawing him fully into the fantasy and reality they were weaving together.

One hand cupped the back of her head, drawing her sweet lips to his, while the other found the curve of her waist and pulled her body closer. Her sweet, wet quim dragged along the length of his hard cock as her hips gave a swivel, pulling a deep groan from him.

Her eyes closed as she released a breathy sigh. When they opened again, they were intent, purposeful. "I need you." She reached between their bodies, and her fingers wrapped around his length. "*Now.*"

Her sex pressed against him, and he went absolutely ravenous for her. But he must hold himself in check. Violet was in control.

Slowly, with excruciating restraint, she slid onto him, taking him in one exquisite inch at a time. Oh, the feel of her.

Her face nuzzled the crook of his neck. "Oh, Will," she breathed, "how can there be yet more of you?"

Unable to resist, he gave a measured, deliberate thrust, seating himself fully inside her, pulling a breathy, "Oh," from her. Her hips swiveled, once, twice, and his hands grabbed hold as she established a rhythm on him. She was so perfect, the feel of her, the scent of her, the touch of her... *her.*

His hands couldn't help themselves as they clamped around her hips, digging in, driving her on him a bit harder, a bit faster, with each thrust. It wasn't enough.

It would never be enough.

Her head tipped back as she rode him, her kiss-crushed lips parted.

"You are a glory, Violet Hotchkiss."

Her lust-glazed eyes locked on to his for a flash before she again lost herself inside her pleasure. Her moans became more insistent, more demanding, her movements more frantic. She was climbing toward release, which only ratcheted up Will's desire.

"Come undone for me, Violet."

"*I*"—she moaned—"*don't*"—she groaned—"*know*"—she whimpered—"*how.*"

Will pulled her to him and put his mouth to her ear, "Your body knows. Trust it." He shifted back and met her eye. "Trust *me.*"

He would take her there if it was the last thing he did.

He took control, clutching her hips, slowing the rhythm, grinding her on him. With each relentless stroke, so, too, did his pleasure begin to build. "Oh, Will," she panted, "I must have... *more*."

"Not yet."

He would continue giving her what she truly needed, not merely what she wanted, thrust after thrust, their breath and sweat mingling as each reached for the elusive place that only they knew together. Her fingernails dug into his shoulders and the increasing volume of her sighs and moans suggested she was close... *so close.* Then she inhaled on a sharp gasp and held, her body locked in tension, before she broke in release on him, her scream of pleasure filling the boathouse, surely rattling its windows. A few hard thrusts later, he followed her, over the precipice into mindless oblivion, his nerve endings delivering pleasure into every cell of his body.

Never had it been like this. A forging of two bodies, two minds, into one.

Inevitably, their bodies slowed and stilled. The only movement was their chests heaving in unison, her face bent into the crook of his shoulder. Even as her breath sent warm shivers rippling through him, reality began to assert itself. There were words he must speak to her, and he wasn't sure how.

He shifted backward, attempting to put some distance between them. She only snuggled in closer. "Violet," he murmured.

"Hm?" He felt her smile against his neck.

"There is something I must say to you."

She angled her head and met his eye. She must have seen something there for the languor cleared from her eyes and she sat upright before scrambling off him. Her lips swollen from kisses, her hair in wild disarray, it was all Will could do not to pull her back in and go for another round. His cock, it seemed, agreed with the idea.

"I... I must dress." She glanced down at his lap. "And so must you."

Will reached down to secure the closure of his trousers, his mind racing. It was clear she didn't want to hear what he had to say. He snatched her hand just as she began to turn away.

Too bad.

She would hear his piece.

"I am more than my impossibly gorgeous exterior."

How strange to be speaking her words back to her, especially those words, but it was important he say them. She gave a nervous laugh, trying for lightness, but her eyes told a different story. They shone serious and guarded. "I know you are."

"And I can be more than that to *you*."

Chapter Ten

Was Will saying what it sounded like he was saying?

When Violet had considered that their coupling was about more than two bodies, had he thought the same, too?

No.

It wasn't possible.

A man like him, with such a gorgeous exterior, didn't have such thoughts about a bespectacled mouse like her.

Violet swallowed around the lump that had formed in her throat as her eye fell on the hand holding hers.

His long masculine fingers. Their warmth. Their strength. He could hold on forever, and she didn't think she would mind very much.

She gave herself a mental shake. She needed to

leave, *now*. She couldn't think clearly with that man in the same room with her, much less touching her. "I shall be missed if I don't go."

She pulled away and broke the contact, determined to ignore the sense of loss pulsing through her.

She gave the room a quick survey. Their hasty progress could be charted by the trail of discarded clothing. She snatched up Will's shirt and tossed it to him. It would be best if he covered that chest of his. As if chiseled from Italian marble, those hard-ridged muscles could distract a lady from her purpose, which was to leave this hut without touching said chest again.

Next, she stumbled across her stays. She slipped them over her head and found his steady gaze upon her. Heavy and hooded, it hadn't strayed from her once. "I, um, need you to tie my laces."

He pushed off the chair, still bare-chested, and deliberately tossed his shirt aside. Without a word, he stalked across the room. Violet turned her back to him, ostensibly to provide him access to the laces, but she knew if his half-clad body remained in her line of sight, she wouldn't be able to keep her reasons for leaving clear in her head.

The breath hitched in her chest when he took up the laces. The silence of the room stretched long and taut as he made quick work of the knot, her skin alive to every brush of his fingers. Once he finished, a sense of self-preservation had her taking a step forward. At last, she could breathe again.

Not another word was spoken between them until she had her dress over her head. "And the buttons of my dress, if you don't mind."

He began to work on her buttons, and her eyes drifted shut. They couldn't help themselves. It was the proximity of him, the closeness of the act, an almost mundane intimacy routinely experienced between husband and wife. It called to a place within her which had only been recently discovered. And a part of her—a rather large part—yearned to explore it further.

Task complete, his hands fell away.

Here it was again. That troubling sense of loss that left her feeling as if a hollow void had opened inside her.

She cleared her throat, wishing other inconvenient feelings could be cleared away as easily. "Do you happen to know the location of my spectacles?"

"On the console table beside the door," he replied, his voice oddly muffled.

She glanced over her shoulder to find him pulling his shirt over his head, fine lawn fabric falling below his waist, obscuring her view of the ridged muscles of his stomach. Yet another loss.

Violet stepped to the narrow, rustic table and found

her spectacles. Once she could see clearly again, she noticed a stack of watercolors. They were Will's, she would wager. She glanced over her shoulder to find him stoking the fire with a bit too much force. A little peek at his latest creations wouldn't hurt anyone.

Curiosity nipping at her, she flipped the top paper over. The figure on the page was a jaunty, monocled pug. Wearing a top hat and blue cutaway coat. Rowing a boat.

Oh.

Violet's breath released with sudden realization. Will had taken her suggestion to heart and decided to try his hand. She held up the watercolor. "You do a remarkable likeness of Sir Pug."

Carefully, Will replaced the iron stoker and dusted off his hands before turning to face her. "Indeed, I should."

"And why is that?" she asked, even as an anxious feeling began to twist through her stomach.

Will cocked his head. "Because I created him."

That feeling in her gut... Deep down, she had known. Yet... "*You?*" It wasn't polite to point, but she couldn't seem to help herself. "*You* are E. B. McWoof?"

Will offered her a bow worthy of court presentation. "In the flesh."

"But, but," she sputtered, "you're *you.*"

Sardonic amusement lit within his eyes and tipped up the corners of his mouth. "Two identities, one man. A marvel, truly."

"But, but," she stammered, her mind singularly unable to comprehend the concept. "*How?*"

"You yourself pointed out my skill in sketch and painting." He shrugged. "And Mother always had pugs. The two came together in my mind that first day when I met you delivering books to the Timpkins girl." He jutted his chin toward the painting suspended in Violet's hand. "I rather think Sir Pug embodies the spirit of the animal."

"But the books? You have bound books." It defied belief, truly.

The blasted man shrugged again. "I know a book binder in Oxford."

Violet glanced down at the painting in her hand. She was charmed, she couldn't help it. "Sir Pug is rowing a boat."

"An idea for the third book," Will said, offhand. "Sir Pug is a consummate rower, except on this day he will enlist the help of one cranky swan to save him from the clutches of a thick clump of reeds and one rather tenacious willow tree."

A light entered Will's eye when he spoke of Sir Pug. He was proud of his creation. And well he should be.

A question came to Violet, one she couldn't not ask. "You should be publishing volumes of flowers and plants. You could be famous in the botanical world. Yet —" She hesitated, suddenly shy of the question she must ask. She cleared her throat. "Yet you've created the Sir Pug books. Why?"

Will's subdued manner fell away, revealing the intensity of the man beneath. "Don't you know the answer to that question?"

Did she?

She might.

An answer which threatened to overwhelm her, even as it provoked another question. Around the lump in her throat, she asked, "How many copies are printed?"

"One of each."

That confirmed it. Violet's heart became a racehorse in her chest, and her skin grew hot. "I... I must go."

It was all too much to think about here and now. In her rush toward the door, she snatched up her pelisse and shrugged it on without slowing.

"Violet, stop," he said behind her, low and commanding.

Without permission, her body did as it was told.

"We're not finished," he said to her back.

She held still. She couldn't turn around and look

him the eye and stay her course. "I need a bit of time."
She hesitated before adding, "Alone."

A few beats of silence extended. At last, Will broke
it. "Take all the time you need. But Violet?"

"Yes?"

"Anywhere I am, you are wanted. *Always.*"

Violet nodded. It was all she could do, such was the
effect of his words.

Then she was moving. Out of the hut, into fresh,
open air where she could, at last, draw breath again.
Across the countryside, she moved on feet racing as fast
as her mind.

Will was E.B. McWoof.

Really, she should have seen it from the beginning.
The man could do anything with a pencil and paintbrush. But it wasn't that fact that had her insides tied up
in knots. There was only one copy of each book, which
meant ... *You know the answer to that question ...*

Will had written the books for her.

It stole her breath away. It made something bloom
inside her that was new and wondrous and frightening.
It was as if every good feeling in the world was swirling
around and through her. But it was one emotion in
particular that wrapped around her heart and squeezed.
It was this emotion that had scared her into flight.

Love.

She had fallen headlong into love with Will Sinclair. Yet one more fact she'd learned on this morning of revelations.

She *loved* Will Sinclair.

It defied all belief, yet it was true. It was the truest thing she'd ever known.

The midnight kiss at the Twelfth Night Ball. The Adventures of Sir Pug. The library wagon. The intimacy they'd shared twice now—in truth, her body was still singing from that last one—these were all evidence of something more.

And she knew.

From the beginning, Will Sinclair had shown her with his actions that he loved her, too.

He didn't see her as a mouse or a future spinster. He saw her as the woman he loved. He desired her—he *wanted* her—for ... *her*.

That life of Lily's, the one that gave Violet short, sharp pangs of envy, the one with a husband, children, and household of her own, was, perhaps, hers for the taking.

With Will.

The hero of her story.

Even as the knowledge sent a joy coursing through her that swelled her heart to bursting, a pit opened up below, threatening to drain it all away. What had she done with his love?

Treated it dreadfully, that was what.

What right had she to the love of such a man?

She had been so consumed by her own goals and desires that she hadn't considered his.

Panic, quick and breathless, assailed Violet, and she started to turn back. The next instant, she stopped. How flighty would she appear if she returned now?

Will deserved better than that. He deserved a woman of substance. He deserved a woman willing to take the same risks for him as he had for her.

Of a sudden, understanding struck Violet between the eyes.

She must risk everything—her pride, her reputation, her heart—to have him, to be worthy of him, for none of it mattered without him.

As the beginning of an idea began to form in her mind, her feet turned toward Granville Court. Lily and Mr. Granville were hosting a family dinner tomorrow night. Lily wanted to have a small gathering before her belly grew bigger than the barn. Lily's words, not Violet's. In truth, Violet thought her sister looked soft and maternal and lovely, the very picture of English fecundity. And, for the first time, the thought wasn't accompanied by one of the tiny spikes of envy she'd become so proficient at suppressing.

Violet would have to persuade Lily to extend an invitation to the Sinclair family, for Violet had a question to ask Will.

And she would ask this question in front of their families and the world, if need be.

There would be no more lurking in the shadows.

She and Will belonged in the light.

He would be hers.

If he would have her.

Chapter Eleven

Will's feet hit Granville Court's gravel drive, and he stared up at the house while adjusting his cravat for the hundredth time this evening. The blasted thing felt like it wanted to strangle him.

Of course, that could be his nerves.

As his father assisted Mother from the carriage, Will questioned his insistence on accepting the impromptu invitation to dine with the Granvilles tonight. Father and Mother had initially thought to politely decline, as it was late notice and they didn't dine out as often these days as they once did. It was Will who had convinced them to accept.

"Have you formed a friendship with Mr. Granville, son?" Father had asked.

Will thought fast, even as he shook his head. "What

better way to grow my friendships with our neighbors than by accepting their invitations?"

"Then it's settled," Mother had stated, final. "We shall go."

Father shrugged his acceptance of his wife's edict—she was the voice of authority on such matters—Mr. Rascal gave an approving bark, and Will released an internal sigh of relief. He didn't give a fig about furthering his acquaintance with his neighbors, but rather one neighbor in particular.

Violet would be attending her sister's dinner, he had no doubt of it. Although he'd thought to wait until she came to him, he couldn't resist this opportunity. The pull of her was too strong.

So, here he stood, his heart racing and his palms sweating like a green youth anticipating a glimpse of his first love. So be it. He had nothing to hide.

If only Violet would see it that way.

The front door swung open and out stepped Mr. and Mrs. Granville, who was clearly increasing. Will couldn't help imagining Violet in a similar state.

"Good evening, Sir John, Lady Sinclair, and Mr. Sinclair," Mrs. Granville called out, radiating happiness and welcome. "I cannot tell you how pleased and honored we are to have you join our little dinner tonight. Granville's second cousin, Lady Delilah

Windermere, has come for a visit, and I thought it would be fitting to introduce her to a few of our neighbors."

Mother's eyebrows lifted. Will knew that look. Mother was preparing herself to be scandalized. "Oh? Is she out?"

Amusement flashed across Mrs. Granville's features. How it reminded Will of her sister. Speaking of whom ...

Discreetly, he attempted to look beyond the Granvilles. His heart gave a lurch. No sign of Violet. Had he misread tonight entirely wrong? Was there to be no Violet?

Wretchedness filled him to the cockles of his soul.

"Do not fear, Lady Sinclair," Mrs. Granville began, "Lady Delilah is out. She simply desired a short respite from London."

Mother's eyes narrowed, her nose for gossip not yet mollified. "Is that so?"

Granville pulled Will's attention with a jovial slap to the back. "Sinclair, good of you to make it out," the man greeted him, all hale and hearty England. Granville was the consummate country gentleman and a good sort.

It wasn't long before small talk turned into genuine conversation between Granville and Father. Will shifted so he had a clear view of the front door. He squinted and was rewarded when he caught movement beyond. The glint of a silver tray, the swish of black wool. A servant. Another arrow of disappointment shot through him.

"Hungry, Sinclair?"

Will turned to find Granville regarding him with a singularly knowing expression. "Pardon my distraction," Will spoke without an ounce of contrition. "I do not recall ever having been inside Granville Court." It was a decent excuse.

"Let us not hold you in suspense a moment longer," Granville said, indicating the group move inside, the speculative glint in his eye not having abated an iota. Will experienced a pulse of annoyance.

Like a good guest, Will filed in at the rear of the group, wondering what he was doing here. Violet was the only reason he'd agreed to this dinner, so if she wasn't—

He stepped into the bright drawing room, and that line of reasoning stopped dead in its tracks.

Violet.

His heart beat out a hard thump. She was conversing with a pale, willowy young woman. He hardly gave the other woman a moment's regard as he didn't know her. It was Violet who commanded his attention.

She'd always loomed so large in his mind that it was easy to forget how small and delicate she was. Someone who had never met her could even assume her to have a retiring personality based solely on her physical form. Until that person looked into her keen, searching eyes. Then one would quickly surmise that the force of her personality and intellect were much larger than the sum of her parts. It was a quality that pushed some away, but one that had always drawn him in.

In all his world travels, never had he met a woman who compared to Violet Hotchkiss.

With a mind of their own, Will's feet began stepping toward her. The movement must have caught the periphery of her vision, for her gaze lifted, slid over, and met his.

The room fell away. It was only him and her.

And yesterday.

Not simply the physical side—although the vision of her straddling him had been the focal point of more than one dream last night—but what had been revealed and what had been left unspoken. It all flashed between them.

The time had come for plain speech.

Will had taken another purposeful step forward when a hand landed on his shoulder. "Sinclair," Granville said, "come and have a sherry. I must hear more about your travels."

Will's gaze held Violet's for two heartbeats longer

until hers skittered away. Left with no choice, he said, "Of course," and followed his host. *Blast.*

Will could hardly pay attention to the words spilling from his mouth as he spoke first to Granville, then to Mr. and Mrs. Hotchkiss, then Granville again, for he was trying to keep Violet in the periphery of his vision. She did flit about a good bit, but never in his direction. The willowy young woman with whom she was conversing had since been introduced to Will as Miss—oh, something or other. Her name was hardly of any consequence to him.

Now, they were halfway through the third of a five-course dinner, and Will could hardly understand how he'd gotten this far into the evening without once speaking to Violet.

"Did you hear?" asked Mother. "Lord and Lady Holland have returned to London to prepare for the Season."

"Oh?" asked Mrs. Hotchkiss. "I would have thought they needed several more months to recover from their holiday house party."

"What a torrent of scandal that was wrought during that fortnight. Even our servants are still tattling about it." Mother might have sounded scandalized, but her bright eyes told a different tale.

"And what a torrent of marriages that followed," said

Mrs. Granville. Mischief curled about the woman's mouth. "A condition to which you must have been immune, dear sister."

Violet, who had been taking a sip of water, sputtered and launched into no dainty coughing fit. Will was about to ask if she needed a good wallop on the back when she, at last, recovered and replied, "It would appear so, *dearest* sister."

"Oh, I'm so disappointed not to have been invited to that party," cut in Lady Delilah. "Well, mayhap not the marriage bit, but for the Twelfth Night ball. I've always believed in the magic of that night." With her direct gaze, Will could see she was no shrinking young miss, but accustomed to stating her thoughts freely. "So, pray tell," she asked, "did any of you observe the scandalous behaviors in question?" Her eyebrows waggled. "Or perhaps engage in them?"

Mother gasped, as she was wont to do at such talk. Mrs. Granville giggled politely behind her hand. Granville gave a stern warning, "*Cousin Delilah.*"

Violet's eyes flashed to meet Will's, a hot blush pinking her cheeks. Their secret shone in her eyes. Indeed, they knew of such scandalous behavior. Further, they had not only engaged in it on that night, but more recently, too.

Strangely, however, Will didn't see fear in Violet's

eyes. He would have thought her worried about exposure. After all, she'd gone to great lengths to keep their dealings secret, even the ones that could be safely uttered in public.

In truth, he didn't know how to read the look in her eyes, which was what had been bothering him all evening. She'd remained strangely closed off to him.

What was on Violet's mind?

"Lady Delilah's elder sister, Lady Amelia, is quite the talented watercolorist," Mrs. Granville said. "Sinclair, it has been rumored that you have a fine hand with a paintbrush."

"Sinclair gave up that silliness years ago," Father said.

Will couldn't help feeling piqued. It was that word, *silliness*. "I still dabble."

He glanced over at Violet, who was regarding him with that curiously guarded expression. He didn't like not knowing what was going on inside that busy mind of hers.

"You are recently returned from travels, am I correct, Mr. Sinclair?" asked Lady Delilah.

Will only reluctantly broke his gaze from Violet, whose eyebrows had drawn together in what appeared to be faint distress. "That I am," he replied. It would be inexcusably rude to ignore the young lady.

"And did you find a great many subjects to paint?" continued Lady Delilah.

"I did."

Will was trying not to be curt, truly he was. But it was a struggle for he had no interest in a conversation with Lady Delilah. What he really wanted was to question Violet, whose brow was now creased into a deep furrow.

"Oh, that must have been a treat," said Lady Delilah, blithely unaware of the stormy furrow of Violet's brow. "What is your favorite subject?"

"Plant life. Flowers."

"Do you allow your work to be viewed?"

There was no help for it. He must give Lady Delilah his undivided attention. The chit was tenacious. "I would be most honored to bring the paintings from my travels to Granville Court for you to see. Although, I am but a mere amateur, so you must measure your expectations."

Lady Delilah gave a delighted laugh. "Oh, I don't think any young lady would have to measure her expectations with you, Mr. Sinclair."

Again, Mother gasped. Again, Mrs. Granville giggled. But it wasn't their reactions that had all the muscles in Will's body bunched in tension.

It was Violet, her face transformed into a thunder-cloud set to burst.

This was it.

The future Violet had always predicted for Will Sinclair was playing out before her very eyes.

And she had to watch.

Lady Delilah Windermere was the precise embodiment of the young lady that she had always envisioned Will Sinclair marrying. With her pale blond hair, wide blue eyes, and tall elegant form, Lady Delilah was the perfect physical match for Will. All one need do was look at them to know its truth. Surely, Nature had created them for one another.

But it wasn't merely the surface of Lady Delilah which was worthy. The lady was irritatingly intelligent and a lively and engaged conversationalist, factors which combined to make Violet slightly nauseous.

She hadn't been able to eat a bite since they sat down to dinner, knowing it was only a matter of time before Will and Lady Delilah discovered each other.

How could Violet fight such destiny?

"Miss Hotchkiss has seen my work," said Will.

All eyes swung toward Violet, even as hers met

Will's across the table. She could get lost in those blue depths for days, which wouldn't do at the moment. "I, um," she stammered. "Yes, I have."

"And how is that, dear sister," Lily asked innocently. *Too* innocently.

Violet tried to catch one of the thoughts racing about her mind. "Well, when Sinclair brought me the wagon—"

"Sinclair, you brought Miss Hotchkiss a *wagon?*"

Although Lady Sinclair was asking Will, Violet felt compelled to answer. "He specially modified it for my children's circulating library."

This seemed to satisfy the woman. "Sinclair has always been a most generous boy."

"But, dear sister," Lily asked, never one to lose the main thread of a conversation, "how did you come to view Sinclair's paintings?"

"He, um," Violet said, "he had some with him." It wasn't precisely a lie. After all, Sir Pug had begun as a painting before he became a book.

"Ah," Lily replied.

Violet knew that, *"Ah,"* of her sister's. Although Violet hadn't explained her insistence on inviting the Sinclairs, it was clear that Lily understood more than she was saying.

"And, Miss Hotchkiss," asked Lady Delilah, "how did you find Mr. Sinclair's work?"

"Exquisite. He has a masterful hand." Violet felt herself blushing at that last part. She knew quite a lot about Sinclair's masterful hands.

"And an eye for beauty," Will inserted, looking directly at Violet as he said it.

Hope cut through the despair in her chest. She'd arranged for the Sinclairs to be at this dinner for a reason. She couldn't lose heart now, or she would lose her heart's desire.

She shot to her feet, keenly aware of everyone staring up at her. Oh, how to begin? "Sinclair and I have spent time together," she said in an abrupt tumble of words.

"Oh, yes, dear, when he delivered the wagon and walked you to the village," supplied Mama.

Violet swallowed. "Beyond that." This was more difficult than she had anticipated. "At the Twelfth Night Ball."

"Well, dear," Mama said, a dismissive tone in her voice, "we all saw one another on that night. 'Tis nothing to become flurried and wrought up about." Her eyebrows met. "Are you quite well? Your color is frightfully high. Please do sit down, Violet."

"I shall not sit down," exclaimed Violet with a bit too

much force. She tempered her tone. "Not until I've had my say."

Seven sets of eyebrows lifted toward the ceiling.

"I've been rambling," she stated.

"Violet has always been a great rambler," Papa said to the room at large. "Ever since she was off leading strings."

Polite laughter sounded around the table, yet did nothing to disperse the tension. They were waiting for Violet to explain herself. Will had sat forward in his chair, his gaze upon her intense and unflinching.

"I have rambled rather all over." Her mouth was dry. She reached for her water and took three big gulps. "On the Sinclair lands."

"Do not feel you must apologize, my dear," said Lady Sinclair. "You are most welcome to ramble all across our lands."

Lily's head canted thoughtfully. "I'd wondered about your recent *rambles*."

Violet wasn't sure how it was possible to have both not enough air in one's lungs and too much. She must out with it. "With Will."

Brown eyes, green eyes, blue eyes, they all flew wide. Lady Sinclair gasped, even as a flabbergasted silence descended upon the room. It was Papa who broke it. "*Will?*"

Papa had caught the distinction, as surely had everyone else in the room. Will was no longer Sinclair to her, and all would know it. "*Will.*"

Next, it was Mama who spoke. "Without a maid?"

Violet gave a nod in the affirmative.

"Cousin Delilah," Mr. Granville insisted in a rush, "I trust that you will speak not a word of this to your mother."

Chin propped on her hands and face alive with rapt fascination over this turn in the night's proceedings, Lady Delilah nodded. "Naught shall pass from my lips."

Papa, for his part, was most definitely not enjoying this, as he'd gone a shade of scarlet that Violet had never seen on a person. "The two of you must marry." His gaze swung toward Will's father. "Agreed, Sir John?"

So, too, had Sir John's countenance gone red, more of a vermilion. "Agreed."

As the four elders, along with Lily and Mr. Granville, begin talking all at once, Violet met Will's eye across the table. Although what she had to say was for everyone to hear, it was truly only for him.

This was her chance.

Her heart in her throat, she tapped her fork against her glass. *Ding-ding-ding.* The room fell into stunned silence. "*Must* isn't why I would ask Will Sinclair to marry me."

Mama gasped. "*You* ask Will Sinclair? Oh, daughter, you have read far too many novels."

"I would marry him," Violet continued, undeterred, "because he is generous and kind and thoughtful. He is as talented and stubborn as he is handsome, which is beyond all compare and measure. Simply, I ask him to marry me because I love him. But only"—she hiccupped on a sudden sob, unable to help herself—"only if he loves me, too."

Will's chair scraped across the floor as he shot to his feet. Heated fervor shone bright in his eyes. "Violet Hotchkiss, I've loved you since before we first kissed."

Lily clasped her hands together, and Lady Sinclair clutched the opal pendant at her throat. "*First* kissed? Oh, Sinclair, where have your manners gone?"

"Mr. Hotchkiss, didn't I warn you?" Mama asked of Papa. "No good comes from letting a pretty girl remain unmarried too long."

"Oh, I think some good might be coming from it," Papa replied, the red fading from his visage.

All this conversation happening around Violet and Will had no chance of touching the air between them, not since they had locked eyes. Will took a step to the side, and Violet mirrored his movement, no care for the others voicing various opinions. Although a snippet about a June wedding did cut through.

Again, Will moved, and Violet followed. They reached the head of the table, facing one another, separated by scant inches of air. Will reached out, and his warm, masculine fingers wrapped around her hand. A smile tipped about the corners of his mouth, and a sigh escaped hers. That smile of his would pull a swoon from her all the days of her life, she knew it.

The sounds of the family fading behind them, Will led Violet through the drawing room and out the French doors leading to the back garden. They walked on until the only sound was the fall of their footsteps and the only light the stars above twinkling silver dots against a clear, indigo sky. As one, they came to a stop, and Violet felt suddenly shy of this man.

Nervously, she broke the silence: "We do seem to find ourselves out of doors a good bit."

Will shook his head, his eyes solemn and intense.

"What is it?" she asked.

"We shall not be changing the subject."

"What subject is that?"

He pointed toward the house. Through large windows illuminated by crystalline chandelier light, they could see the family, still discussing them, lit like figures in a water globe. "The one begun in there."

Violet summoned the bold resolve that had carried her this far. "That I love you?" she asked.

"Aye." A smile curled up one side of his mouth. Oh, how she wanted to kiss it. "And that I love you."

The words—to hear them set free on the breeze—stole Violet's breath away.

"You are brave, Violet."

"Hardly. In fact, I rather think I've been a coward."

"What you did in there took no small amount of courage."

"Will," she said, needing to say this, "I treated you poorly. Can you forgive me?"

"I've nothing to forgive. What is it the Bard had to say about the course of true love? It *never did run smooth*?"

Now Will Sinclair was quoting Shakespeare to her, as if she'd harbored any doubt that he was the perfect man. "Will?"

"Yes?"

"Will you marry me?"

"It seems I must."

"No, not because you *must*. Not because of what our families expect."

"Oh, but I absolutely must," he confirmed. "My heart and my soul and my body dictate it so. You are the one with no choice, Violet Hotchkiss. With your declaration, you've made it so 'tis *you* who must marry *me*."

"Pardon?" Violet couldn't help feeling the events of the evening had been turned around on her.

Will took her face in his large hands. "Violet, you are mine, and I am yours. *Forever.*"

She lifted to the tips of her toes and linked her arms around his neck. She breathed in his warm scent of sandalwood and man. "Forever might be long enough."

"I have my doubts."

Will bent his head and claimed Violet's lips in a kiss that she'd been waiting for her entire life, the one that sealed her forever with Will Sinclair.

Epilogue

Florence

"Do not move."

Violet smiled down at the letter from Lily that she'd only just opened and settled into her perch on the windowsill. She had grown quite accustomed to this command from her husband.

"This early autumn light is perfect," he said, the raspy scratch of his charcoal pencil across paper sounding from across the room. "Your skin, dear wife, possesses a luminosity that only oil paints could do justice. I may have to find a master to teach me the medium."

A warmth and love swelled up inside Violet that she didn't think she would ever become accustomed to. She focused on the letter in her hands. "Shall I read you the news from home?"

"If you must," Will replied, distracted.

He'd told her on their wedding night as they lay in bed, still panting from the love they'd made, that wherever she was, was his home. All she'd been able to do was nod, so strong was the emotion that surged within her. Even after four months of marriage, the feeling hadn't lessened a bit. If anything, it had only grown stronger.

She cleared her throat. "Lily sends her regards to you and says that all our parents are doing well."

"Good to hear."

"And she goes on at some length about baby Charlie's feeding and sleeping habits." For two pages, front and back, in fact. "But she asserts that all his feeding has given him the most delightfully pudgy, pinchable cheeks in all of England."

"That is important in a baby."

Still reading the letter, Violet chirruped with sudden laughter. "Oh, you must hear this."

"If it is regarding baby Charlie's nappy habits, I shall be content to let that stay between sisters."

Violet gave her head a shake, the smile on her lips only broadening. "That's not it at all. It turns out your cousin Mr. Quincy has gone and fallen madly in love with Lady Delilah Windermere."

"Oh?" Will's lips were turned down in concentration on his sketch.

"And apparently Mr. Quincy was so inspired by our dinner declaration, that he stood up and announced himself besotted with Lady Delilah in the middle of a village assembly."

"I wish them every happiness." It was apparent Will wasn't the least impressed.

"But that is the thing," Violet continued, unable to contain another chirrup of laughter. "Lady Delilah laughed. Not out of shock or delight, but a laugh from the depths of her belly, according to Lily, which went on for a full minute, which Lily emphasizes is a very, very long time in such a situation. Anyway, after Lady Delilah settled at last, she stated a simple 'No,' and after a shocked minute of silence, which really dragged on, again according to Lily, that was the end of it."

Will barked out a loud guffaw. "What a dolt. Public humiliation can only be good for Quincy. Never know, it might be the making of him."

Having dispensed with all the relevant news, Violet set the letter aside. She gathered her silk robe about her and stared out at a Florence awash in golden light. "I believe we must return to our little corner of England, my husband."

How she loved calling Will Sinclair her husband. It gave her a fleeting thrill every time.

"Must we?" he asked on a low rumble, the majority

of his attention focused on the figure emerging beneath his hand.

"We must."

His hand stopped mid-stroke, and his gaze lifted, eyes questioning. He'd caught a note in her voice. "*We must?*"

"It's really too bad you can't get both of us," she said, pointing toward the sketch in his hands.

"I'm no good at self-portraiture."

"Oh, I'm not speaking of you."

Now was the time.

Violet placed a hand on her stomach, which had grown ever so gently rounded. For a short time, she'd thought it a consequence of all the wonderful food she'd consumed these last few months. Not so, it turned out.

Will's pencil dropped from his hand. "Violet," he asked, a slight wobble in his voice, "what are you saying?"

"I think you know."

He shot to his feet, his sketch materials scattering across the floor, forgotten, and rushed across the room, gathering Violet in his arms. "Are you certain?"

She nodded, her eyes welling up with tears of happiness.

As she melted in Will's arms and his kiss, she marveled at this life—and this man—she'd somehow attained. A hero not of pen, paper, and romantic ideals, but one of flesh and blood and heart and soul.

A real man.

A real life.

All *hers*.

And to think it started with what was to be only a kiss.

Lady Amelia Takes a Lover

Windermeres in Love Book Two

By Sofie Darling

Chapter One

Florence, Italy, March 1820

"All we need to do is behave," said Lady Amelia Windermere for the thousandth time to her sister Delilah and cousin Juliet.

Speaking of misbehaving... Amelia turned her head this way and that and still couldn't understand precisely why the pomegranate set so prettily beneath a window refused to flow from her brush and settle onto paper like a good little watercolor.

"It's only for a little while longer," she added.

It was too much to ask that the Windermere brood behave for an indefinite amount of time. Still, she could sense eyes rolling toward the high, airy ceiling. It may have been spring in Italy, but their rented three-story palazzo held the perfect temperature, allowing gentle breezes to drift through at will. While not much was superior to her homeland England, she might have to consider that the Italian weather was. Most of England would've been soggy and cold on a late-March day like today.

"Shall we behave like Archie is behaving with his opera singer in Naples?" asked Delilah, reclining lazily across a plush velvet settee the rich hue of sunburnt earth, mischief in each syllable. Amelia didn't need to look at her sister to see it in her eyes, too.

"What happens in Naples..." Amelia wasn't quite sure where she was heading with that sentence. It was the red, she decided. The pomegranate red wasn't quite pink enough. She added a dollop of water to the paint mix.

"Stays in Naples?" added Juliet, ever a wit with wordplay and seated near the open doors that led onto the terrace. She'd positioned herself so as to better catch the afternoon light for the book she was reading.

Juliet had come to live with them after her parents had perished in a tragic carriage accident when she was but aged two years. Though a second cousin once removed, she was as a sibling and was treated as such.

"I cannot behave, Amelia," proclaimed Delilah. "You might as well toss me into the Arno now."

"Delilah," began Amelia, sensing one of her sister's dramatic moods coming on.

"What's the point of being alive if you can't truly *be alive*?"

"Delilah—"

"One's soul shrivels into nothingness."

While Juliet might have a way with creating words, Delilah had a way with speaking them. One felt perched in the palm of her hand until she'd finished. It had been so since the moment she'd strung a two-word sentence together in her baby cradle.

Still, as the elder sister by five years, Amelia knew when to put her foot down. "Delilah, I forbid you from throwing yourself into the Arno."

Her sister stared moodily out the window overlooking said river. Delilah—like all Windermeres—didn't have the natural mien for brooding, with her crystalline blue eyes and blond curls that streaked platinum in the summer sun. "My soul might demand such a cleanse." Byronic the Windermeres weren't, but Delilah was giving it her best impression.

Ever the pragmatic one, Amelia felt it her obligation to point out one important fact—the *most* important fact. "We shall never be received into polite society again."

"It would be the leap too far," said Juliet, provoking a giggle from Delilah and a reluctant smile from Amelia.

"But we *are* received in polite society," continued Juliet. Where the Windermere siblings were all curly blond hair and blue eyes, their cousin Juliet had straight black hair and clear green eyes so direct they could see into one's soul, or so it was suspected by all who met her. She had, however, inherited the famous Windermere height. They were tall to a one.

"Oh, dearest Juliet, have you learned nothing from this past year?" asked Delilah, wide-eyed and innocent. "You are speaking of polite *Italian* society, and Amelia isn't. She's speaking of the only society that matters to the English." She allowed a laden beat of time to lope past. "Polite *English* society."

"Well, I think the Italians are very nice." Juliet shrugged one shoulder and returned her attention to the book on her lap. She always had a book on her person. She even had a special necklace with a notepad attached. Juliet was serious about her words.

"Delilah," said Amelia, her brush only now making headway with this baffling pomegranate. It was the blasted texture of the thing that was trickiest to convey with a watercolor brush. "You aren't being fair to the English, or the Italians, or me. I would like to return to London and be invited to all the balls and soirées. Is that so wrong?" She glanced up. "Has the post arrived yet?"

Delilah and Juliet gave each other a sly look that said they knew exactly why Amelia had asked for the third time today. "I don't believe so," said Juliet.

The thing was Amelia had a plan to rehabilitate the Windermere reputation and slip back into the good graces of society before their parents, the Earl and Countess of Cumberland, returned from their two-year archeological journey to Samarkand. Mama and Papa need never know that their children had fled England with scandal nipping at their heels, rather than for a simple holiday.

By Amelia's calculations, that left them another year; but if all went to her plan, she and her siblings would be enjoying the highest society of the *haute ton* within three months. The plan was simple: secure an invitation to the Marchioness of Sutton's ball that marked the end of the season in early June. A cousin had assured Amelia the invitation would be arriving by post any day now. But Amelia wouldn't believe it until she held it in her hands.

And now Delilah was threatening to throw herself into the Arno.

Being the only sensible Windermere wasn't the easiest lot.

"But here's the thing, dear sister," said Delilah. "*You* want to be a lady."

"I *am* a lady." Amelia pointed her paintbrush at Delilah. "And so are *you*." Her brush shifted toward Juliet. "And *you*, too."

"I didn't choose to be a lady," said Delilah. Oh, how

she loved to say that. "In fact, it's a great hindrance to what and who I want to be."

Amelia released a long-held, long-suffering sigh. "What you want to be, Delilah, is what landed you and all of us out here on the fringes of polite society in the first place."

Delilah directed her unflinching gaze at Amelia. "All you need is a paintbrush and paper to create your art."

Here came Delilah's grievance, which Amelia had heard a good seventy-three times, if once. While she had sympathy for it, she'd long lost patience with it.

"All Archie needs," said Delilah, "is a pianoforte. And, Juliet, all you need—"

Juliet held up a staying hand. As ever, she preferred to stay clear of Windermere sibling arguments. "I have no artistic talent to speak of."

"—is paper, pencil, and a chair placed at the periphery of a room for your art," finished Delilah.

Juliet's smooth brow lifted. "And what art is that?"

"Listening."

Juliet scoffed. "Listening isn't an art."

Delilah snorted. "The way you do it is, and don't think I haven't noticed." She stopped long enough to draw breath. "And *I* need a stage and an audience."

Amelia let her brush fall to the table. Now it was her turn to voice *her* grievance for the seventy-third time. "But did you need as public a one as Eton College?"

Delilah shrugged her shoulder.

Amelia wasn't finished, for her grievance was never satisfied until it had a full airing. "And did you need to pretend to be a boy pretending to be a girl pretending to be a boy to do it?"

Delilah looked at Amelia as if she'd suddenly become the most stupid woman in all the world. "That *is* the role of Viola in *Twelfth Night*."

Amelia's eyes rolled toward the ceiling and remained there until she'd achieved a measure of calm. "But it's the bit where you pretended to be a boy to get the part in the first place that society has taken issue with."

How many times had Amelia pointed out the distinction this last year?

"Eton is an all-boys school," returned Delilah. "How else would I have been able to secure the role?"

And how many times had Delilah refused to acknowledge the point?

"And to think Archie helped you," said Amelia. She still couldn't believe it.

"The bet was Archie's idea in the first place."

"You didn't have to accept."

"Sometimes, it's like you don't know me at all," said Delilah, exasperated. "Besides, Archie's been wanting to get one over on Eton since he left however many years ago."

"But you, Delilah, are a lady of two and twenty years." How many times had Amelia pointed this out? Oh, yes, seventy-three. "How did you ever expect to succeed?"

Delilah snorted. "The haircut helped." She ran her fingers through short blond curls.

"We shan't discuss your hair," said Amelia. She still hadn't recovered from The Haircut. Delilah had once possessed the most beautiful head of hair ever beheld, rivaled only by Amelia's own long blond curls. Only Botticelli's Venus standing on her half-shell held a candle to a Windermere head of hair.

Juliet lifted her head. "I rather like Delilah's haircut."

Oh, dear cousin Juliet... So honest... So annoying.

"Lady Caroline Lamb would approve." Delilah knew precisely how to fray Amelia's last nerve.

"*I* think it makes you look like a twelfth century monk," said Amelia. "Without the bald patch, of course."

Delilah and Juliet shared a conspiratorial snicker.

"Further," Amelia couldn't help continuing, even though she really, truly shouldn't. "Lady Caroline Lamb's approval is the very last thing this family needs."

But Delilah wasn't finished torturing her sister. "I

could procure a straightedge and give that bald spot a running start."

"Don't you dare." Amelia had to say it. She never quite knew how far Delilah would go.

Delilah's mouth curled into the mischievous smile that ever did get her out of trouble with her older sister. "When did Archie write that he would arrive?"

"Tomorrow." Amelia picked up her brush and resumed her study of the pomegranate. It looked…angry. Perhaps she was taking out her frustration with her family on the poor, blameless fruit.

"Which means he could arrive any time between now and next week," Juliet pointed out.

True. The Windermeres ever had a loose relationship with timekeeping.

"Oh, by the by, Amelia," said Delilah. "I've decided I shall attend tomorrow night's soirée in honor of the Duke of Ripon."

"Didn't you say soirées celebrating decrepit, old dukes weren't worth your time?"

"Don't forget *lecherous*," added Juliet. "She said that, too."

"I said *likely* weren't worth my time," said Delilah, indifferently flicking a piece of lint off her skirt. "And as none of us have ever clapped eyes on the man, as reclusive as he is, well, I'm curious, and in need of society and prosecco."

Something akin to dread filled Amelia. If Archie did, in fact, arrive tomorrow, the possibility existed that the Windermeres could be attending a society function all together—which hadn't happened since they'd left England. Which meant, of course, she would be playing nursemaid all night, because, quite simply, her siblings couldn't be trusted not to be utterly and completely themselves—charming, but improper and slightly scandalous, in either word or deed or, most like, both.

A feeling jogged on the edge of memory as if...as if she was forgetting something important, like an...

Appointment.

All-too-familiar panic seized her. "What is the time?" Time just never seemed to pass in the linear fashion everyone said it did.

Delilah pulled a pocket watch from the discreet hip pocket she had sewn into all her dresses. She'd explained it was something about being an actress and timing and honestly Amelia hadn't been able to understand the reasoning. She couldn't bring herself to give a fig about time. Signore Rossi, her Italian art instructor, did, however.

"Five minutes shy of one of the clock."

"Blast!"

In a frantic rush that brought mean, little smiles to Delilah and Juliet's faces—they'd heard that exact exclamation regarding this very topic more times than any of them could count—Amelia gathered her brushes and palette and shoved them into her valise, which she grabbed on the run. "I'll be back in a few hours."

Muted laughter followed Amelia as she dashed from the palazzo and onto the street, her feet a rapid tattoo against cobblestones. The scents and sounds of Florence crashed into her in a frenzied rush, as they always did as she crossed one square, then another, flew down a labyrinthine maze of alleys, another square, then it was a quick turn onto a narrow street, an even quicker turn into a quiet alley. Twenty steps later, she'd arrived, panting, at the turquoise-painted gate of Signore Rossi.

Taking no time to compose herself or wipe the sweat off her flushed brow, Amelia planted both hands on the gate that led into an exterior courtyard and began to push when it suddenly gave way and an ox plowed into her, knocking her off balance and flat onto her bottom, her skirts forming a white muslin puff around her—all in the space of two seconds.

She held a hand to her forehead and glared up at the ox.

Well, not an ox, precisely. But an ox of a man, to be

sure. She couldn't see his face as the sun was at his back, creating a halo of light around his massive hulking form.

"Please don't apologize," she said acidly, dusting her hands off on her skirts, before checking that nothing had spilled from her valise.

The man snorted. Rather like an ox. "That was far from my intention. Perhaps it has occurred to you that you're entirely at fault for your current condition."

"Why...why..." she sputtered through righteous, disbelieving shock. Never in her life had she been spoken to thusly.

And she most definitely didn't like it.

He held out a hand, presumably to help her to her feet. She would rather grab hold of a writhing serpent.

Gathering the few remaining shreds of her dignity available to her, she managed to scramble to her feet with her modesty in place—*thank you very much*—even if her bottom had begun to throb. It wasn't until she was squarely facing the ox of a man—well, not *facing* precisely as he stood a good six inches taller than her and she was no diminutive woman—that a shocking fact hit her. "You're an Englishman."

And a noble one at that, given the clipped syllables of his speech, even if his appearance lent a different impression given that he was wearing the clothes of a laborer and his brown hair hung unfashionably long and loose about his face.

What sort of English nobleman was this ox anyway?

He grunted—like a grouchy Highland coo she'd once encountered in Scotland—and that was leave taken as he brushed past. A faint blend of scents remained—clove, sandalwood, and... Was that *sweat*?

Tetchy remnants of the encounter quaking through her, Amelia entered Signore Rossi's exterior courtyard and halted, dipping a hand into the fountain depicting frolicking water sprites and bringing it to her face. She needed a quick cool-down before greeting Signore. What just happened?

Servants accustomed to her twice-a-week arrival simply nodded as she slipped through Signore's typically Italian palazzo and into the studio, with its tremendous north-facing windows that allowed light to pour in at all hours of the day. She found her customary easel and began readying her pencils and brushes. A bowl of fruit had been arranged for her session today. Perhaps not the most exciting subject, but a useful one in her education, of course.

Still, how many bowls of fruit had she painted in her life?

The lot of the gentlelady painter.

Signore Rossi and his little white dog Dolce entered

the studio. "Ah, Signorina Amelia, you decided to join us today." He ever commented on her lateness—as was his rightful prerogative—but did so with a smile on his face.

Dolce curled up on his purple velvet pillow across from her, allowing sunlight to soak into his scruffy white fur, his little face resting on a paw, gaze lazily fixed on outdoor happenings in the cypress trees. Amelia found herself doing a sketch. Just a few lines to expand upon later.

Signore glanced over her shoulder. "Ah, would you like to paint Dolce today?"

"*Si*," she said, already delighting in the prospect. She rarely painted live forms with Signore.

She attempted to quiet her mind and enter the creative space where her brush would find inspiration for this little moppet of a dog. But she was still fizzing with her collision with the ox. Before she knew it, words were spilling from her mouth. "I just had the most curious encounter at the entrance to your studio."

Signore Rossi didn't bother looking up. "Hmm."

"With the most incredibly rude man."

A name, she wanted a name.

All Signore gave her was another, "Hmm."

She wasn't to be put off so easily. The ox was a menace and an Englishman. She couldn't let it pass. "Is he your student?"

She had to know.

Even as the question passed her lips, however, an image entered her mind. Of his hands, unrepentantly massive and masculine, like the rest of him. She couldn't imagine those hands holding anything as delicate as a paintbrush. Surely, it would snap in two.

Signore Rossi set his charcoal down and gave her an indulgent smile. "Signorina Amelia, would you appreciate me passing your information along to all manner of those who might ask about you?"

There was but one answer, and it put her in her place. "No."

Signore nodded, and that was her question sorted. She wasn't to know. She was to forget the ox of an English nobleman whose face she hadn't clearly seen.

Dolce shot to his four feet and gave a sudden round of barking at the squirrel who had the temerity to race up the cypress nearest the window. The little dog was on high defensive alert.

A chirrup of giggles escaped Amelia, and her brush sparked with inspiration. She would call the painting, *Our Greatest Defender*.

As her brush followed the creative muse where it led, oxes of men were forgotten.

For now.

Also by Sofie Darling

Windermeres in Love

Mr. Sinclair Beguiles a Bluestocking

Lady Amelia Takes a Lover

Lord Archer Catches a Contessa

Miss Windermere Woos a Highlander

Lady Delilah Dares a Duke

All's Fair in Love and Racing

Odds on the Rake

The Duchess Gamble

Wager With a Siren

Devil to Pay

Win Me, My Lord

A Lady's Rogue to Ruin

Shadows and Silk

Three Lessons in Seduction

Tempted by the Viscount

Her Midnight Sin

To Win a Wicked Lord

At the Pleasure of the Marquess

One Night His Lady

Nell and the Runaway Duke

About the Author

Bestselling and award-winning author Sofie Darling's passion for historical romance began in middle school the moment she cracked open *Wuthering Heights* by Emily Bronte. An instant and enduring love affair was born.

Sofie spent much of her twenties raising two boys and reading every romance she could get her hands on. Once she realized she simply must write the books she loved, she finished her English degree and set pencil to paper. (Ticonderoga #2 is her quill of choice.)

When she's not writing heroes who make her swoon, Sofie enjoys a nice weekend hike, a visit to a crumbling medieval castle whenever she gets the chance, and a slightly codependent relationship with her beagle, Bosco. Visit her website.

A small press bound by the belief that every voice matters.

Sign up for our newsletter to learn about new releases and more.
https://oliver-heberbooks.com/subscribe/

Follow us on social media:

www.ingramcontent.com/pod-product-compliance
Lightning Source LLC
Chambersburg PA
CBHW032306310726
48973CB00008B/2536